HONORABLE

HONORABLE

Purpose in Repose

KATHRYN GRANT

TATE PUBLISHING
AND ENTERPRISES, LLC

The opinions expressed by the author are not necessarily those of Tate Publishing, LLC.

This book is a work of historical fiction. The names, descriptions, and incidents are based on true stories and actual historical figures.

Published by Tate Publishing & Enterprises, LLC
127 E. Trade Center Terrace | Mustang, Oklahoma 73064 USA
1.888.361.9473 | www.tatepublishing.com

Tate Publishing is committed to excellence in the publishing industry. The company reflects the philosophy established by the founders, based on Psalm 68:11,
"The Lord gave the word and great was the company of those who published it."

Book design copyright © 2013 by Tate Publishing, LLC. All rights reserved.
Cover design by Anne Gatillo
Interior design by Joana Quilantang

Published in the United States of America

ISBN: 978-1-62902-126-3
1. Fiction / General
2. Fiction / Historical
13.10.31

AUTHOR'S NOTE:

Born a slave as Providence planned, Lucy Higgs Nichols was snatched from her mother and sent south, still an innocent child. Risking everything as a young woman, she escaped in 1862 to save her only daughter the same destiny. Documented evidence of her tenacious struggle from slavery to freedom exists. Indiana's 23rd infantry gave her refuge near the onset of the Civil War. Eventually revered by these same men, she served as nurse, cook, and laundress to their advantage in almost 30 battles from Tennessee to Washington D. C.

After the war she still marched to the beat of her own identifiable drum. Settling back in New Albany, she continued to nurse sick vets back to health and work in the homes of various officers. Honorable "Aunt Lucy" became the sole woman ever unanimously elected to the GAR (Grand Army of the Republic) by soldiers. Official papers researched record her life, one of four black women known in history to receive their government pension after nursing during the Civil War.

This fascinating story is based on true-life events. Upon reading an article about Lucy in the *New York Times,* more than 30 years after the Civil War, spirit spurs a has-been writer and war veteran to seek out this woman he's never met and help her share a story of heroes. He chronicles a tale, of intrigue, romance, and adventure, which recognizes God's purpose for them both. Eloquent witness and healing through faith are nurtured along the way. Surviving years of war, illness, and setbacks with courage, truth, and heart Lucy outshines intense prejudice and unstable politics to impact and inspire mothers, nurses, and soldiers beyond repose.

PROLOGUE

Of thoughtful consideration, my cached cup commonly sits half-full and remains. Our nation's erstwhile war created a backlash of burdens wearing in weight and troubling to toss as cargo from an overloaded freight. Positivity's position drains. Amidst the bravest of soldiers, slaughtered in a red swath of bravado, bathing the battlefield in blood, my attitude for artistry fell dead with the same. Imagination's muse, now muddied, became a heaving anchor beside fallen friends and sank darkly in the sludge, stuck in deepening furrows of my unseeded and faltering faith. Why was I alive, unmaimed? I managed to muster out at the end nevertheless, looking lame as a limping amputee, not half a leg, half-sane. Shot somewhere in the ambition, a crippling malaise, just when after the war, I cannot say. The wound was insignificant compared to losses compatriots sustained, worthy brothers who never returned from an opaque fate. Dare I disgrace them with my paltry complaints? I was listed on a ledger of the living, a survivor of the uncivilized, civil war game. As a participant I marched with men and heralded hurrahs at heroes' parades, but decades fell away and my spirit did not rise like a phoenix from the ashes unscathed. A gaping hole in my heart ached for purpose; but instead, as if pierced by my own bayonet, held scars and pain.

I yearn to find existence with an honorable purpose and strengthen it as to me, my country, and my faith proclaims, yet no intentional knock of opportunity came. Left to ascertain my own reflection, I paced in a tower fully self-made, clothed in the pitiful costume of an ostracized misfit to be shamed. When reality roused suspicion with more than a few eyebrows raised, an emotional debt collector pounded on the door of my soul demanding pay. Broken in spirit and surly, susceptible to blame, I shut the door retreating in spades. Albeit ugly in retrospect, apathy's head too more fully raised. Blithely taking aim at an opportunity to stay sane, Thanksgiving's irony reigned. Oblivious to a situation sullied by my condition I addressed my public without refrain and in denial as a lost dog wandering astray.

I engaged the invitations' outing anyway, conscience outvoted. By society's gourmet standard, mussed hair needing a trim, disheveled suit needing the flat-iron, imperturbably retied and badly knotted boot laces, my appearance tasted rather unsavory; far better received at home alone. At first pass, piquant companions and approbating loved ones goodly goad in uncontained, sniggering groans. Counsel's advisement to change course structured status quo. The conversations continued throughout dinner at a cordial, comrade's abode. Appurtenant in arrangement, variously tenor and baritone voices pearled around tightly knit café stools, primed antique armchairs, and clinked cuffs on stuffy, brandy snifter sofas. The staging, however cozy, portrays an overly relaxed and comfortable tone, not so. Men of certain ages saddle-up often for intellectual entertainment, a showdown which engenders, un-reined and uncontrolled, smashing reprisals of "braggadocio en debate politico." To us it speaks distinction, more rightly than an evening beside the new-fangled radio.

Constrictive as the life-ebbing boa in manner, but regrettably noticeable only to those I let close. I felt as if I sported a ball and chain anguishing the ankle and flailing with a clunk to the floor as each step goes. Despite intervention's intermission, spiritually I begged to be unshackled, but the anchoring stone remained in tow. Pale and stymied in solitary salute by the window, I turned to leave stiff and austere as Andrew Jackson immortalized in statue, bereft unto a taciturn, empty tomb, till returning home. There, my nightly reading, neglected atop the bedside table, begged caress as words of spirit can oft console. Tonight's offering immovable, no splendid solace was sown. Rejected pages blankly indisposed, offered no softly evening succor to cover me with Whitman's perfect prose.

Let us digress in discussion, pointing out the political body's core to fully explain. Since 1851 partisan influences were best held apart in a fist fight, piqued on prospect at the odds and diametrically belayed. I as well felt punched to provocation, more personal than a rogue wrangler trying to rope in my patriotic outrage. Now '98, the penchant for barely covering unsettled arrears to federal fighters objectified American aims, not unlike the mass grave at Vicksburg, which coddled a risen stench for years, came as a cry of shame. Intentional anger, rightly displayed, smolders within families like hot coals await the poker's thrust to reignite a flame, but smother in ashes and niggle at sides, despite the losing hand having been dealt and played. Veterans suffer after economy's death-blow and subsequent pain. Waste not comment on the emotional casualties' foray, nor expound on multiple and tragic mutilating, dismemberment claims. Do I exaggerate—Nay! Solemnity suffers, spot-on with reconstruction on the wane. "Lady Liberty", France's gift of glory, a lit torch for freedom's fame, becomes the backdrop, a prop if you may, the only tragic figure adding grace to our stage.

Embattled Lincoln's phrases, not yet a motto made; see us stand in mourning, years older, yet civility more or less the same. We mature less and bluff more about bastions of freedom, thereby inciting combustible, incendiary blame. What shall ignite the impervious catalyst to spark racial change unashamed? Did God in all His glory and grace unbeknownst to me become renamed? Does it assist to consider from whence we came? How do we not question collateral, moral condition in decay? Are fingers crossed, when we pat surviving heroes with earnest embrace? A country continuing contrary at cards could lose its shirt gambling in the rapidly declining, poker-faced game.

Instability still waxes colossal, increasing unrest and the armistice further at stake. Marshaled troops called to cities, a hard won peace is not kept in place. Other factions of authority sally a strokes by poking fun and pulling down shades, when marauding reactionaries' wanton, welcome is overstayed. Skirmishes garner anger's girth from pockets of people infecting terror with an acrid, guerilla tactical reign. Homeowners too, harbor grudges, like drought invites wildfire scorching a path aflame. Not in deference to war's wounded remuneration or avaricious tastes, as one might think is the case. Folk of this nature ooze indignation's sass like a festering sore does ache. We, as unskilled social surgeons, are highly doubtful afforded opportunity to amply amputate the same.

Wrists insipidly slapped, pay likely encouragement not to disband or dissuade. Folk forego formalities to erupt inimical and volcanic effrontery ensues like sub-terra munitions blasting a barbaric shock to common challenge government control tries to dictate. Irascible as crabs scuttling sideways on a shifting sandy bay, they reach not for gold or even stars and stripes, but selfish, grudge-holding gain. Their single-minded purpose creates scars and pushes like an icy glacier to mark generations with a deeply rutted vein. God forbid the weakening resolve wanes and their objective barrels broadside against their own compatriots in pain. Hear the begging meek cantor, "God keep us sane." The Great War, ever-lasting to some, is indelibly etched above tallies on blocks of an invisible prison wall sentencing psyches to unyielding disdain.

The additional tally of which I'll speak more plain, refugee slaves, spread bare as a tsunami wave unbuckling ashore to an unprepared inland main. The imbroglio of oppression gives America weft, yet the warp proves too unwieldy to quickly weave segregated folk into the wake. The southern, migrant tapestry tainting war bleeds color like unwoven threads led astray. Howbeit, I dare not say. Though initially unfettered in some states, dignity for many former slaves was caught in a rat-trap of law, which chokes the folk who dare to nibble at freedom's cheese gone stale and thus, not assimilate.

Observed by Webster's see-sawing value of what's humane, selected gentlemen express interest tongue-in-cheek and ease their approach on reactionary reins, yet beneath their face is a soul's abhorrence for every human's God given rights to the same. An abolitionist purveys these issues in debate: 1. Folks of that nature are morally root-bound, entangling sinister ethics at the psyche's base. 2. They have simply run off the reservation and disappeared round the bend insane. Do people brought to our shore by inexorable inclusion deserve exclusion, the ethics bound disparate? Ballyhooed, impassioned cries were once cohesive, not so long ago interlaced with America's unique charm to unite populace. Now careless, carousing rabble cackle greatly. Cluck, clucking various exacerbations in fractured, castigating cliques denying ridiculousness with callous "beg-your-pardon" strains.

I will myself to write, rather than talk about our country's internally bleeding wound of racism, but by what means do I capitulate? A malfeasant fate boasts on, lassitude to its own undoing in baleful berate. Vacillating I'm stayed, too stuck in the boot sucking muck and mire of the musty main to create. Weakly wavering, perseverating knees shake and bend as I splay on the unforgiving stone to pray. Shall I braid to Divinity and beg kindly Grace, prone on the floor of my quarter's dismay? A whispered plea weathered on my belly-crawler's bottom of 1898. What if I don't ingratiate the greater good God would make? As the lunar crescent smiled through dusty panes, I looked upward to the Throne of Grace.

"What, Dear Father in Heaven, shall this man do then in purposeful service to ingratiate?" I heard a small voice inside my head, "There are no mistakes."

December 14, digits dove in '98. Though an exceedingly nippy morn, I never forewent my usual corner café's coffee and newsy perusal of the day. Haphazardly, I nabbed my nubby scarf and encircled my neck like a noose on the way. Insatiable charity did not delay. The New York Times netted a boatload in admirable dark print for serendipitous parlay. Enjoyed alfresco, an article flew up on the gale catching my gaze, "Pension for Lucy Nichols," "Noted Woman Warrior," in a paltry paragraph display.

Unknown racing out the gate, I began the journey to save my soul that day. Spirited energy slowly saturates desire like cream sliding down berries atop teacakes, my hungry pen dips into the well salivating to create. Providence praised! I will find this "woman warrior" of uncommon fate and kick start the catalyst of dominoes in chase of change by telling her tale. Is it not reasonable to anticipate? Does not the honed spotlight on hearth-lit hope held to a hero's humble face miraculously impact souls, more profoundly than surface graced? Absolute truth sternly knit persuades the likes of Harriet Tubman interviewed by the Ray Stannard Baker template. Determination unraveled at an obscene pace. Nevertheless, four months preparation carried on to set the stage. After arrival in Indiana by noon train, a driver took me to Naghel Street, where the cottage nestled on a seemingly insignificant lane.

SOVEREIGNLY POINTED

Greeted by the gate with a creak at the rusty hinge tweaks my ears like the elderly rising I confess. Prognosticating tension holds its breath, shuttling me back to shy in earnest embarrassment, since introduction's professional care had sung out in discordant announcement. Entrance toward the porch pulses to hesitate me midstep, upon hearing the unoiled, improper pronouncement, but an odd mix of incisive hopefulness happens at that same moment, profound and unexpected.

Leading my visual, greeting pansies perk to attention and exhilarate. Slender, soubrette stems bow at a hardy howdy-do in hind quarters' array. Ruffle-skirted petals curtsy at the splendid sun, always amenable to liberate. All are joining in a dance to the hum of early rays. Bronze butterfly snapdragons bear open, virtuous, yet agape. Their silent ohms mysteriously articulate fragrant hints, which visit the upper monasteries of the nose, spicy and understated. A colorful choir's observation to the naked eye I must say. Nature surveyed kindly, welcoming to the strangers and known visitors alike, albeit unplucked, a blossoming bouquet.

What if a dowdy dowager waits? A propensity toward possibilities gave way to pretentious, nervous bane and crashes ashore my mind like a stealth, midnight wake. The sidewalk seems to lengthen my sashay, but my overreaction at present is pleasantly replaced. Inches from cresting the porch stair the sparkling sun shows its face. An unfiltered examination of personality enhances curiosity to set the stage. I aim straight for her eyes and encounter grace, sincerity, and warmth emanating. Punctual as reveille, she did not give a snappy soldier's second to waste.

Within my brain the assurance of a reporter and an author's insecurity amalgamate. Is Lucy Higgs Nichols the personification of an indemnity initiate? Propositions posit acutely serious, but I, flying by the seat of my pants as yet, had not planned this practical, paradigm change. Not that I advocate perspective reversed in haste, but guileless consideration for the mind and heart to revive, or shall I say to resuscitate. My tableau, bent on deceptiveness, had mental pictures of her frame, previously cut and pasted. Valiance like the Valkyrie may have suited her name, but fully mortal she came, right as rain. Her actual inclination was conservative in demeanor, drawing proper weight. Not a reclusive fascinator, but reticent and actually preferring chaste anonymity of late.

Monumentally multiplied in conviction from the start, I was immediately put at ease by her uninhibited candor and graceful art unabated. Youthful in the hanging umbrage of the roof of the stoop, a sable hand harbors near the screen door ajar draping at the end of an aging arm. Salt 'n' pepper, woolly locks crown her head with a cluster of charm. They whiten where widow's weeds took root and chart life's rockier parts. Those wiry tresses are mollified in traditional convention, a simple chignon sluiced tidy and smoothed back with a midline part.

Clattering and briskly poking past the brim, battering the metal with a clackity startle, the other pushed a cane through loosely attached on a crocheted chain of yarn. The wristlet was deft, homemade-smart. The cane's handle pauses with a slant, perching temporarily taciturn in poised testament told to an old porch wall, slightly sad-sacked, a photographer's vintage, cover art. Notation on a mental card, the whitewashed-paint spoke of a provisional, brittle-skin... torn years discarded, flaking and sun-scarred, competing in adherence with each upset of life's applecart.

Lucy conducts an incumbent salute before countering resolute toward one of the porch, rocking chairs with a courteous grin. Though her shoulders tolerate the sufficient slump of sixty, her eye brows raise up adequately to acknowledge me again. Invariably compelled to return, I sent out a morning grin directionally before sauntering the gravely-patches of the path wearing thin. Customary pleasantness in manner most always passes the bowl of butterbeans table width to chit-chat, never a mind to verbosity or wearisome wit. I draw on genuine banter's best to aim for acquaintanceship. Buttressing discussion tit-for-tat, tête-à-tête via positive regard, breeds familiarity built in pendulum swings.

ROCKING
CHAIR'S VIEW

"Blest mawrnin' t'yuh as yuh's movin' on through. Don' mind tow'rd me, till I gits muh angle t'improve. I be ans'rin', easy as yuh please, t'pahrslin' d'pawrch view. I got's t'point muh chair t'suit d'eastuhrly aspec' fo' sittin', a spell sawrly due. Puhrspectif do come mawr pyuhr wif a careenin' backw'rd sawrta move, much t'antis'pate d'Lawd's show.—Free thin' t'do."

The surprising vim catches me a touch off guard here. My ears echo with her hope for the best in everyone everywhere. Boldly, she still holds fast to conveying optimism in life dear. Crossing my legs, slightly square as a primitive desk, I adjust a loose-leaf book, prop a pen and gently nod at the amenable atmosphere.

"How do you do Mrs. Nichols? Please give my regards to Mr. Hooper, your former employer, for assisting with introduction in our affairs. Many compliments to the perfect array of flowers you've got there."

"Thank yuh kindly fo' sho. I be much oblige to 'im ovuh d'yeahrs in tow, but he done remove t'Denvuhr, wuhrkin' fo' d'railroad long 'bout ten o'twen'y yeahrs ago. Yes suh, I do love watchin' d'flawuhrs grow."

Lucy attests with an elated eloquence to relax any shamble of nerves, still trying to have a go. "Now, I declare! T'share a mawrnin' greetin' an' sich'ate wif d'sun's smile gives yuh a glow. Why, lo 'n' b'hol', it jus' spread out like some spectac'lah fan dem ladies spawrt in dancin' shows. Ain't no bettuh way t'wuhrk in a pair o'boots o'stahrt d'day b'fawre d'cock crow! 'Minds ya quick as a snappin' whip what d'impawrnt thin's be in tow; 'gahrdless o'whar yuh ahre o'whar yuhr due." She nodded her head in her own agreement. "Phew, so true dat,—so true! Doncha know? Gospuh shahrp, Pastuh Roguhs, truss me up like dat a-whuhrlin' win' o'yeahrs ago."

Vulnerable wood on the chairs had become weathered, nebbish and care-worn, beaten down by seasonal elements in brutish, changeable turn, as too did the bleaching sun's drying light. Curving arms and legs bent oppressively are smoother at the grip, wearing well the weight of life. Tolerable rocked to the tiresome core of contrite particulars—doggedly back and forth each time. A stalwart disposition hammers hickory against might to stay resolute. Lucy's spry, slender fingers squeeze and release their grasp on resting rails' iniquities and accomplish indelible marks imbued. Wanting reassurance, her weak knees unfold languidly complacent, outdone by unruly creaks of rotting porch planks, which balk and weigh in with elderly dispute. After a lingering angular lean causes composure to bear on the balls of her feet, a hint of risen heels lifts as if on cue. Tingling whisks to toes in faded, buttoned boots and crinkles with a-wiggle in her forward reel due.

Gently rocking to and fro in the chair frees a few fleeing, wispy strands undone from her bun to blow with the air. The troublesome tendrils seem to sweep aside a current of cares. Left forefingers corral some strays behind

an ear and then brush past her mouth to muff a minis-
cule, childlike chortle escaping there. The sight gives any
frown repair like watching a tittering, young patron snare
a circling painted pony at the county fair.

"Lawd fawrbid, if'n I's not t'share yuhr uhrly, watuhr-
coluh sky, still upliftin' fain' 'n' bri'yant hues at libuhrty
wif fahr away cares." The tempo resigns to a flirty fanning
for her face, submissive fingers nimbly flair. The flick of
Lucy's willowy wrist swishes flies and activates a flourish
of musical beats with a soothing sway across the air.

Famously familiar, melodious in refrain, the carol cod-
dles senses to a tissue and lolls tenderly rare. A lilting,
gaseous trail of notes meanders effortlessly up Heaven's
invisible stair. Sounds seem to suspend and undulate
through the atmosphere, iridescent as the rainbow in
misty spray midair. Singing old hymns refreshes the
seminal mustard seed of faith in an unabashedly, ageless
affair. If anyone dare prove profuse and powerful existence of Providence, it is then and there to share.

"Der it go' ag'in—like a-heahin' from a deah ole frien'.
De cawruhs o'dat heav'nly hymn, Amazin' Grace, keep'
a-comin' t'de fo' by 'n' by, yet mahrvelous, anew. It be bref
takin' as a-ticklin' toes in d'grassy, daybreakin' dew."

Creeping closely to the rocking aft a contented, short-
haired feline meticulously licks white socks clean. It slinks
in with a slow, "S" shaped tail switch and a puny mew fit
for the meek. I am awestruck at a neighborly and picturesque, panoramic scene. Burr oaks, fatter at the trunk
and thicker in the bark from spring's burdening rains
are obese and arch across, framing Nagel Street. Milder,
in measured communion, a black maple releases angel-
winged propellers, which dive off occasionally twirling

lazily down to discard seeds. Two sedate sumacs bolster like stately bookends, towering over a few white dogwoods bursting blossoms inside the lower edge of foliage, a grander map of peace I have yet to see. Powdery petals from the swirling flowery clusters frolic on a delicious breeze, quite the resemblance to snowflakes on flight's fancy in irony. I surmise it to be midspring's generous sighing desire for falling mercury.

In that instant's observation I join the un-stirring pair on the porch, downright tongue-tied. Twin breaths unify twixt hostess and her feline pal to pay serenity homage. I must say, they appear quite harmoniously allied. I chose not to misalign their insulated existence in a perpetual push for interviewing participation just yet, feigning time to bide.

"I once was los', but now I's foun'." She purrs with a Mona Lisa smile. "Lawd, have muhrcy! I sho be d'livin' proof!"

The metronome rhythm maintains, goodly worn into proven grooves, whilst Lucy independently sings and ritually scans north to south across the neighborhood.

"Well, look a-heah!—Jus' ovuh der, out d'cawrnuh o'muh eye, flappin' fo' glawry t'save dey lives, espy three, white buttuhrflies, one o'God's bles' gif's. Cat jus' nigh musta flush't 'em from d'thickit. Why, der dey go, still a-fancy flittin'."

I hear a soft tsk-tsk beckon sooty-furred mittens with pink-padded under paws to playfully tap at threads dangling from her skirt by the hem. Sympathy is a sucker for milky mews and receives the requested grin. A coy caress against a porch edge submits thankfulness from his whiskery chin. Lucy shakes her head to adoration's allegiance and the hymns' swift surrender. Resuming mid-refrain ends the notable tune in an unassuming, fawning inflection to her compact companion's esteem, as if thereby the animal agrees to permit.

"Was blind, but now I see." Lucy hushes to a softer, finishing refrain, elongated at his consideration. Fluffing up a white-feathered breast in fashion, a woodpecker rears back in appreciation. His passionate reverberating pecks on a mealy maple trunk descend with a whinny, possibly desirous of a duet with dueling instrumentation.

PRESERVATION'S EMPATHY

"No, I ain't from 'roun' dese pahrts 'rigin'ly. Though Indianny be d'place I stakes muh claim, I's bawrn due eas' an' souf' Tenn'see raise'. Reckon dis heah's whar I come t'res', amids' a bevy o'folks what knew me bes'. 'Cawrse we came t'be like kin,—well, mawr o'less d'same. Dose brave ole boys from Indianny's 23rd endeah me t'Aunt Lucy durin' d'war one day. Dat time t'dis be what dey come t'callin' muh name." She says it with a touch of twinkle, when she looked my way.

"Most dose men gone t'dey grave', but I reckon we meet ag'in on D'Judgemen'Day. Till den, I tries t'membuh what I can an' waits. When we gits wif d'Grand Ahrmy o'Republic fo' meetin's, we rec'lecs dem days. Lemme see now, whuht I's gonna 'membuh t'day. S'pose what's not impawr'nt I won't rec'lec' an'way."

"D'Good Lawd 'low'd me t'travuhrse dis heah Erf a ways, mahrchin' fahr souf o'dis lan', back tow'rds muh birf an' toppin' nawrthuhly agin.... a time o'two, ev'n though dat be deceivin' t'pas' decades o'hist'ry in priv'ledge avail't. Seein's as pres'ntly, I's livin' like a ship adock wif no awrs o'sail. Cawrse, now I stays well 'bove d'line o'Mason Dixon fame fo' goodly reasonin' jus' d'same."

"See, I come heah by no easy han', ev'n pond'rin' a fair bit t'take a stan', yet whils' I sit. 'Mind yuh don' heed fife 'n' drum t'de freedom call, a-cockin' 'n' a-rockin', whenevuh y'awll see fit. Unsung heeruhs… t'mah accoun', stay' d'cawrse through untol' glawry—fightin' d'good fight wif guts 'n' grit."

"I come by way o'Nawrt' Car'liny, back 'bout 1838. Folks say dat I be bawrn dere, but I ain't 'memb'rin' d'date. Some say sich thin's don' mattuh much fo' d'slave, but sho as I'mmuh sittin' heahr, awll thin's has reas'nin' in God's gran' play. B'fawre infuhrnal battles be b'ilin' knee-high-bloody 'n' hawrse t'full heat, ev'n ere I growed t'pull a weed o'grab a root t'eat, muh mammy was a slave, a-cullin babes dat came due chain', sol', o'seal't. Yes suhr, I growed up in d'days o'chattel, fahr yonduh dis heah place. Twas d'life o'de slave-bawrn chile dat come t'a-vouch muh uhrly fate. Contemp' 'n' unscrup'lous scoundruhs take t'concil'tatin' sens'bil'ty tow'rds sich states o'unres'. Only de Good Lawd, Hisself carry d'scahrs t'heal 'n' save dat misuhrbuh mess."

"I s'pose muh humblin' hist'ry I shares like mos'ly folks do. If'n I pare back d'presen' like onions cut t'stew, I ovuh-trace hap'ness, sadness, an' d'folks I knew. Lawd willin' jus' may be places in sharin' 'n' repairin' dose broke' bits, some drea'ful—just drea'ful dispar'gin' too, gives dem boys honuh, so sawrly due. Be mo' dan jus' a soul-sketchin' mem'ries.—It sho 'nough be dest'ny, tried 'n' true!"

Dissuaded distal aphorisms of vintage vines around old memories vie and untie metaphorical yellow ribbons from a forest of toughened emotions falling mute to the wayside. Magnanimous character curtsies a cue for the curtain to rise on a heroine's tale trapped no longer, neither denied nor tower entombed and trapped to abide.

"Thin's come t'me in spells, yuh know," Lucy professes a dusty disclaimer to ride.

Nostalgia overbears sparks of earthy gold cascading outward, a kaleidoscope of honey-hued colors enlarge the buff-brown irises of her eyes. Hesitating a second of momentum, her head cocks to the side and psychoanalyzes. The hypnotically pendulus chair pauses, stalling on a situational tide. The halt upholds an underpinning of courageous carriage and brings with it testifying witness on the rise.

Peculiar glints surface, inklings to youth's former ardent pitch. Lucy's nostrils flare to sniff for a quickening burst of breath, chin-up, adjusting her neck taller, an attentive appearance, but more relaxed within. She exhales tenable to regained shards of wit.

"I be seein' sumpin," Lucy informs me of her inward expedition arousing my interest in curious, bilateral bits.

As if she is going to whisper, I turn a leaning ear, espousing a listening posture's cup, not to lose a drop of the story dripping through. Her eyes shut to spawn a penetrating search endue. Sparse, black lashes blink, when unsparing memories span another shivering second or two and arrest Lucy with a serious, dour flinch at thoughts imbued.

Calm as a fisherman at the pier, I wait patiently, bait to hook. My expression, composed, reassuring by the book. A choice to push forward or take leave stands precarious in the face of a naysayer's look. Well known in newsy circles, when unleashing a story to the public, judgment wears like a faux pas jewel about the neck and begs folks to look. Thusly, daring to hedge presentiment it hangs for all to view like a sandwiched-sign spouting guilt in a shamed roué mistook. Similarly, soldiers bare chalky letters abreast to display the piratical, mutinous "M" or the deserter's "D" but we, not knowing their heart, thusly prey as exemplified rooks. Do we all have buried treasures of tales to explain the twists and turns our life's journey took? If given time to explore the past, explanations eventually bubble up, biting surface-wise from a wellspring in the archived nooks.

Past an angling change from the splendid sun's rays, I presume to wait on of significant wage. A less routine, cajoling rock of the rails engages. I wink, grin, and nod okay, acceptance of her sixty-odd years' suffrage. We both sinal with an smile, nonverbal, understood scrimage. Time snails away on the page waiting for what she will say.

"I ain't fo' wifstan'in' d'amoun' o'news in muh yeahs, but placin' d'blame squarely t'muh age."

I'm not trying to sell a bill of goods. A life story of substance cannot be muzzled by the newsmonger's shrift or spoiled by some pushy or selfish, investigative crook. This type of telling could neither be ballooned by a speech in some prodigious general's chronicled report nor penned on the page of strategies in a Civil War book. Heroes found behind the scenes are never trifles to lay aside as undesirable or mistook. Lucy fought to survive the Civil War unforsook. When a precious voice testifies to truth, it should be treated as a treasure with more respect than just a haphazard listen or a passing look?

Now in the land of hope, I'm choosing to pitch my tent. If wind-flipped pages of an antiquated book were sentient, magnanimous motion would slowly sweep across codified sentiment. I could see the wheels of preservation turning to bygone years and doors to the past press open, gnarled in past design with cobwebs of conscience most urgently spent. Her river tossed mysteries soon reveal themselves as we pan for golden gems. They sit sequestered on a shelf, statuettes like fragile figurines glassed in a curio cabinet. No, not deliberately, for venerable gaze, heretofore locked as they stay; but a pampering, sacred pain the soul and mind have saved, lined with a velvety, permanent silence. They subsist in spirited testament.

Lucy carefully cradles emotions like early evening fireflies gently kidnapped under a glowing grasp to watch them blink beneath the covering of the other hand's hollowed compartment. Pratfalls and pitfalls presaged, even perfunctory peeks coul risk precautionary measures, which bind a child's regret. They grip the ledge with fingertips on a wall of inner innocence and an emotional bend, considered best forgotten. No angel unaware she embarks on her journey like a cicada readying its wings on a branch after casting off its restrictive shell. A serendipitous spirit pulls back the sash and sheds light on her pilgrimage. Lucy emboldens in steps, slow as blackstrap molasses.

"Twas...dis...away... Aftuh d'longes' dry spell we's evuhr t'see at Grays Creek estate..."

IMPERISHABLE LESSON

"I's ball't up like yestuhrday's 'needs-a-washin' an' th'owed on d'unfawrgivin' wagon bed. Reckon, Mammy, done give me up fo' dead o'say I suit muhsef fo' showin' a-saucin' spir't instead.—Fo' days boun' t'pass, but sleep done keep me from knowin' what time be lapse'. Sees as muh gut gonna speak up—'bout two days, since I's fed las'."

February's chill at dawn is the source of a foreboding, distant cock's crow. A singular shudder snags little Lucy from her pleading subconscious for a longer, healing sleep. Wincing, eyelids constrain against an abrupt sunshine's baking offensive, slapping her cheeks adumbrate like spanking spurs jolt a stubborn, unbroken filly's flanks. Rude wagon jounces from pesky wheels bump in and out of an unscrupulous rut, precisely calculated to interrupt file, and charge the ranks, until hoof or wheel topples kaput. The even clip-clop of the shoddy mare trips in strut. Impetus recovers him soon enough with a whinnying mane flip, a neck nod, and a nostril snorting nose jut.

Beligerence hails insults upon the impertinent situation paramount to ignorance and insolence, which further jade. Mightily jarring the little fledgling fully awake, the flashback from the farm smacked her again, sullen and sunken, drunk with dismay. The ensuing alertness inveighs ever increasing aches endured from antics participated in a day and a half before; dead like the opossum deem more susceptibly played. The tip of Lucy's parched tongue touches a trickle of mature blood on her lip, dehydrated, dusty and caked. No speaking or movement, are a last ditch vestige to control advantage on approach … a ruminating vexatious coil in the corner, motionless as a mannequin from a shop window cast away, arms awry on a store's cellar floor after giving time displayed.

"See, d'stahrtin' o'de fracas be,—when muh olduh brothuh 'n' sistuh, Aahr'n 'n' Ang'lina, git rope-tie' like a coupluh o'mules t'be sol'. Dey's stahrk resign' t'de ser'ous stroke o'dol'fuh grief come t'wretch kin from fam'ly in a mannuh o'unspeakabuh woe. Dem's d'hokum I ain't yet t'know, but I's feelin' sumpin balefuh 'bout t' hap'n in muh bones.

Wif a might sorruhfuh face, if'n truf be tol', I be scrabblin' 'n' fussin' like a squealin' swine dat don' know which-a-way t'go. A-high-tailin', scare't rabbit I be hoppin' 'hind muh Mammy' an' grab't huh skuhrt like I's a boat in tow. Thinkin' like a mulish chile tryin' t'hide from cho'es. Maybe I be thinkin' Mama' ain't gonna make me go…" Lucy reaches up in a punching, acrimonious clutch at the air with both fists shaking pugnaciously, shoulders tightly scrunched, and chin hunkering down as if invisible, jail bars held her brazen effrontery, but indeed, there was no place to hide.

"I be like a Blue Ridge tick on a dawg, plum dug muh feet in place an' stuck hol' muh Mammy's skuhrt tail…" she trails off, her fists and shoulders relax into the safety of present day. Fingers flip forward flush and then up with hands slowly out-flung in accepted disbelief and dismay. Lucy adds eyes askance, her neck tilted into her shoulder, while pressing lips firmly together in acquiescence to a society gone culturally cold and gray.

"Awll d'othuh slaves be awatchin' t'see what gonna hap'n nex'. None gonna uttuh a wuhrd o'let out d'smawlles' bref. Dey jus' keep on stan'in' like dey's stone, cow'rdly, hex't. Tied to, Aahr'n 'n' Ang'lina be starin' vacan', a sadly, kinda disconnec'. Eyes wide like great, beahrded bahrn owls, puhrchin' on a limb t'inspec'… Yuh know, like d'innuhcen' deahr aftuh dey know dey shot—big, black eyes dahrkly puhrplex't. Dey's shock't mawr'ly monstrous, unfawrch'nate kind o'sorruh dat stab down t'de bone mawrruh in effect."

"Mammy jus' press huh han's t'muh face," 'Lawd keep muh chillin safe.' "I sees huh teah as she say dat kinda hush-a-bye like, lookin' wif love an' he'pless disahrm awll d'same way. I be shakin' muh head, sayin', No! Mammy, no, but she step off wif dat sol'tar' teah, moufin' wif no soun'… 'Pray, baby pray.'"

An uncivilized welling in my eyes crests; helpless therein it stays. Incapable in that moment of an ambiguous or ambivalent notion at the insidious treachery, I bite my bottom lip inside to keep my focus straight. Even my mighty fountain pen falls flaccid on the page, comatose in concern upon the notebook, for what to say.

Lucy checks her cheek with fumbling forefingers to dry a tear-trail gone astray. The ambient greenery no longer assumes massage of the day, so I offer a fresh hanky, which upon a thankful nod, is gently brushed at bay. Obstreperous, childish displays of improprieties now cogitate, notwithstanding reticent rejection of the pusillanimous, I pat myself forehead to cheeks before I tuck the hanky, unable to comfort, away.

"Ole privy stinkin', mealy-mouthin' drivuh try t'snatch muh hands 'n' yank' 'em t'de rope. I bucked 'n' catywault cleahr t'de nex' coun'y, kickin' up quite a bullheaded row. Den as if I stealt cawrn from d'Massa's sto', dat eevuhdouh haul back t'give me a blow 'n' tan mah hide like I's a pesky, black crow. Mad as dem hawrnets come out d'hive a-buzzin' t'oppose, full fo' a fight, doncha know?" Her right fist ratchets a few goes. Mayhem bruises black and blue in riposte of indignation's whirling tornado, against the youngest maid's derisive trope.

"Yuh know how a black bear take t'thrash a vahrmint; paw goin' backsmack t'scol'? He done cuff't squawre 'side mah head an' whack't me out col'.—Down t'de groun' I go Unsuhr'mon'ously, I's tol', he pick't me up an' toss me like a rag'dy doll on d'unfo'giv'n wagon flo'. Fuhrs' time dis heah Negruh feel love gone col' like someun done peel't d'appuh an' toss out d'very cohr'. A mighty weight drap' full on d'scales o'muh soul. He be ridin' d'tippin' p'int o'decency draggin' d'flo' like a wagonwheel o'life done broke an' lef' me stranded fo' d'juhrney home"

Purity once possessed years ago is now stolen treble fold in the punitive incident and dashes Lucy's ego, stunts her mind, and drives the dirty development over her soul like a speeding motor car. Downtrodden and stymied in spirit, they're earmarked. Chattels in tow cough and chafe on shock-laden puffs still suspended above the road on a fine-silt bar. Emptiness dredges up and up in the air, bragging loquacious about the hard day's embezzlement with a thicker, dust-choking chimney tar. All those watching as well are marred mentally and become mired in the tramping of childhood's joy meant for life's journey at large.

Epitomizing the episode charged emotions run rampant and raw, but whispered among the farm's slaves, a tarnished replica of economy's barge-bogged par. Mississippi mud quickly built up on bare toes and crusted in the crevices hard. The dampened spirit wears a badge of hard-knocks. It commiserates to the unpleasant alternative, while trekking twixt a southern border beyond from Higgs' farm. Soon enough, the episode is filed under cautionary card. Shifts idle heavily mum and retarded. Grim movements equally weighty are girded worrisome to restart. For a time the marauded rucks are regarded to needle nose motes, regrettable and sad as a south bound mouth made clear shaven, they remove miles afar.

Usually, a slapdash ruckus sends most folks aback; a view of rambunctious behavior as such or likewise a cacophony of drama can hit one's sensibilities as rash. Thusly existing, a bruhaha can extract complexities of loyalty and surrender to bury memories under an avalanche of agony like a snowy, wintery passage. The pain pops out unpredictable to sting like sizzling grease from a hot, griddle pan. Straight-lipped and unmoving Lucy and I sit to process petulance. We relive and reimagine a licentious man behaving brash, whilst the darkly distant reminiscence evaporates as cinder's ash.

"Bless mah agin' soul! Dat chile's hahrt be so heavy. Thinkin' like a li'l gal los' from dey mammy in d'mahrket squawre. Hain't been apahrt dem five o'six yeah', nary a sweat-in-yer-eyes' blinkin'. Sting smahrtly longuh too, stronguh dan a switch' whippin'."

"Fo' a spell I be still—listnin', 'ceptin' fo' a pinch… I stole a steely ganduh at dat buhrly, bullyragguh on a ruff'un's seat-o-sin. He twarn't werf a mouf full o'tatuh ashes gone col', but dat ain't no mattuh den. Stahrvin' awll d'whils', I's feelin' empty like a homemade coffee can drum stretch't wif pelt a dry skin. Ribs so pawrly thin, I's rustlin' like cawrn shucks a-dryin' in d'aust're, autumn win'. Cawrse, in dose days, d'fattuh d'hogs, d'leanuh d'slaves, dat be d'way a-thin's. 'Ceptin' nothin', but ahr bon'age, till we was in d'graves, derein be d'reasonin' I growed up dat day wifout stretchin' so much as a hog's tail inch."

"Dog muh cats, aj'tatin' impuhdence ain't change fo' suhrcu'stance—neithuh hol' a broke' hahrt fo' healin' nahways. 'Twas sich a lil gal, but I lern't silence be awll d'mo' gol'en d'hahrd way. From den on, I's no longuh quahr'lsome an' do what d'white folk say. I gits t'hobblin' my lip 'n' cawrk' up d'quiet way.—'Vench'ly, a bendin' bow gonna break."

Expatriate of enemy influences, Lucy, audibly dejected, exhales. Fatiguing stories donate to the waxing shade and a morn heading stale. Off the leafy line of maples and beeches, I see her stare at the neighbor's yard; safe harbor of present day brings blood to the brain and a face gone slightly pale. Her left palm positions across her right over the well-worn, white apron, pocket edge dog-earred tired, tattered and frayed. A press up to full attention loops the wristlet and wraps fingers round the hackneyed-handle of her cane. With a cursory glance I notice three lines engraved, a dozen or more men's names. Given as a gift … solid reminder of soldiers Providence saved.

Before I could comment an attitude of mum conster-nation comes mindful of manner. An ephemeral pursing pout and flaying cluck follows with a couple of shakes to and fro frm her petite-coifed bun add to prior the dis-play. Lucy, clearly dubious of contextual contention, thins her lips, knits both brows and stands a spell to shift her weight and reevaluate. She studies transcendent trees and ceases a discerning gaze with only the left brow raised. No words amply animate.

"I don' 'membuh much 'bout d'nex' 'two o'three yeahrs in d'Miss'sip' state. Maybe it gonna be like chaff t'de t'reshin' flo', jus' d'same. I tes'ify it be a powuhrfuh time a-weepin' fo' a-needin' muh mammy, fo' hahrshes' toilin', an' fo' d'mis'ry a dearf' 'n' deaf' t'come an' change muh ways. 'Vench'ly, I tuck't up muh boot straps an' 'membuhs t'pray, kneelin' full t'whispuh on d'flo' tow'rd d'en' o'each day, jus' like muh Mammy say. God ansuh prayuh sho 'nough, when down d'road come a toluhrble pahrlay."

"D'young Miss Win'fuhd Higgs take lame from a coughin' mis'ry inside d'yeahr an' pass on t'de grave. Now I ain't awishin' ill on her, seein' she be in d'ohrphan way. Lawd knows, we 'bout d'same age. I sho nuff be like de ohrphans, mammy gone, ain't no pappy t'speak of nah-ways. See heah, Massa Rueben Higgs fuhrs' wife remove' t'Miss'sip', when der marriage lay in waste. Soon as y'awll can spit, **she** go an' pass on t'de grave huhsef in haste. God save us awll, 'bout d'same time *he* do dat in Tenn'see … like some strange, white folk one-uppin' game. O'cawrse der ain't no joy in folks dyin', but d'Good Lawd may have a chuckuh o'two in His gran' plan, jus' d'same."

"Likely full-on brutish, dat cuhrmudgeon, Wheelin', be lyin' awll ovuh tahrnation like d'spies double-talkin' outta bof' sides o'der mouf in some trav'lin' med'cine show craze. Dey hahrpoons sawrry folk dat's gullibuh 'n' vuhn'ruhbuh like goin' aftah one o'de Lawd's sheep dat strays. Higgs ain't in his name! Dat' awll I gotta say! Praise d'Lawd fo' a new day! Cawrse, dat ain't stoppin' him from commencin' t'scheme nahways." Lucy's index finger waggled to indicate accusation as she swiveled her eyes swiftly up and to the right and cocked her head with a braying disdain.

"A palav'rin' prattle distuhrb' rathuh considuhble jux'apose Higgs' kin an' unctuous Wheelin on accoun' o'who goin' t'own d'slaves. I'se Higgs…like muh mammy. Slave folk 'n' prop'ty takes on d'Massa's name. Cawrse, flat stones skimmin' back 'n' fawrf cross d'Hatchie don' unbreak peace, when a foo' t'blame."

PURPOSES TO EACH

Lucy courteously pours us a couple of cold drinks in her serviceable fashion. For the neighborhood kitten, a crust of day-old bread cut up in bite-sized bits soaks in a small saucer with a taste of milk. Catering to fill, a creaky-handled ice-box, eager enough for famished morsels within, holds fresh milk, bottled, three brown eggs, dappled, creamery butter, a slightly soft, half-stick. Homemade, sweet tea to suffice in the poorest potter's pittance of a pitcher drips from a dime-sized chip at the lip. Spotless and orderly on minimum bill, her home does not seem a stitch out of place; of course rapid view permits a limited run of the mill.

Hostess hospitable, she returns with a grin and trusty treats hoisted aloft. Rusty from exposure, the screen door opens and closes with raspy, haunting half-measures concluding with a "FOP". Resonation that spends nerves like musket shot. Her elbow knocks a drop from the kitty's dish spilling the whiteness in a spit-sized dot.

"I swat," Lucy falters acknowledging nerves caught. Unfazed, shrewish mewing pitter-patters to the top step and continues on the stoop, in delighted dialogue. Placing the old, floral-patterned vessel foremost receives adulation in grateful pleas, which finally succumb to a motorized hum and mellows before the shrillness stops. The tiniest tongue rapidly laps the last drops.

"Slow down der, if yuh will; bettuh t'make dat las' a bit an' relish dem vittuhs down d'road a piece."

Her left hand trembles, a weakening wrist quiver left unanswered, which tallies further fragility, when put to the test. She flattens on a small, heart-shaped locket holding a tiny shock of course, black hair to her palm's heated flesh, as if instinct impels her to protect, when sleeping memories surface afresh. The piece of Lucy's unsung past hangs on a thick, cotton thread. Three fingers from the quaking hand gently tap twice upon her chest.

The tumbler of sweetened tea nestles in a middling groove of the pinafore over her dress between both hands cooling the palms' flesh. She steadies the glass with her mid-west, ladylike manner at its age-mobilizing best. Lucy sniffs and gambols unstressed into the story's next section, more at ease and affable, since finding unalloyed joy over each slurp of her pleased partner's snacking mess.

"I ain't meanin' t'wish dyin' on folks, much less d'likes o'de young'un, Miss Win'fuhrd un'er d'guard'un o'Massa Wheelin. Mo' likely, I be prayin' d'Lawd gonna take me outta dat mess."

Humanity's moral compass slides on a slippery slope to compare. Countless countrymen justify the shuttling of slaves from master to master like the bearish market of trading shares, senselessly separating families, downright deplorable and unfair. Bartering for men, women and children like sunburnt mares without so much as a bye or leave from here to there. Lucy could not contain the incredulous vehemence she had welded into an emotional shield to bare. Like the gnashing teeth of a growling wolf garish and avaricious owners profit well from the atrocious process, even down-pared. Brigands, bandits or any other bodies trading and selling humans have no compassion; the almighty lure of money is their only care.

"Massa Wheelin' sich a snake in d'grass. Why dat swindlin', triflin' cuss, cain't be trusted nahways. We's sho as shootin' t'fall prey t'de likes o'huhr quick'ning en' an' untimely fare."

"Now, dey go' on 'n' on, fussin' 'twixt dose Higgs kin an' d'Massa—'bout us, an' how dis heah 'stablishmen' goin' t'run,—but once d'tussle said 'n' done, I en's up wif Mawrcus, Massa Rueben Higgs' ol'es' son. D'worl' in Tenn'see ain't stop a-tuhrnin' dem yeahrs I's gone neithuh. As I trus' in Jesus—fo' muh life ain't yet begun. Cawrse, slaves by d'hun'erts, poss'bly thousan's, allus feah d'south. Folks get dey spir't snatched from d'likes o'seethin' hahrt's mis'ry priuh t'de time d'Lawd gonna take 'em t'de grave, awll d'mo' reasonin' a judge gotta decree t'ahrb'trate ahr fate. D'acquittin' reprieve be what I prayed he gonna say. Inside d'nex' yeahr der we be, headin' back nawrt' t'de Tenn'see state. I reckon 'twas three yeahrs t'de date. We's shucked back t'differ'nt ownuhs, wuhrkin',—'twas d'life o'slaves."

"Truf' be tol', I's jus' glad t'be shut of 'em. Dem's d'meashuh o'vahrmints 'n' skallywags dat wants t'net slaves like dey's a sorry shoal o'fish t'fill d'buck'neah's boat. Dem's d'pahrates o'de seas dat use't sell folks like dey's pyuhres' silvuh o'gol', 'spesh'ly, if dey's on d'platfawrm t'be swap' o'sol'.—Dat be d'case, unless folks be ole. Cawrse, massas takes 'em inta dey fol' like scare't, squealin' shoats an' wuhrks 'em wretched, right down t'rotten, till dey's a scragglin', nag hawrse, fall't flat, feet up-roll'd."

The red-veined, yellowish whites of Lucy's eyes protrude as she looks up inside her lids, momentarily sticks out her tongue to hang low, and flips her palms up and under in two swift curls, fingers flush, and wrists bent skyward to suggest a nag's culling dolor be told. Wanting to change the subject, I asked about Marcus Higgs, the next on the list entrusted to one of God's own.

"Fancy dat Massa Mawrcus, 'bout dat time he up an' go find a Kentuck' gal t'chuhrch vis'tin' kinfolk. Soon nuff, fo' yuh knows it, he hitch't. Move' fo' a while on down t'Miss'sip' wif huh'n t'ado' an' Aahr'n 'n' Ang'lina in tow. I nevuh sees muh kin agin ya know. Mawrcus Higgs sign off t'low me t'stay in d'Tenn'see way. Praise d'Lawd! Dat always endeah him t'me fo' sho.'"

"I's hire't as a house slave, t'cook, scrub, 'n' hep unduh d'teachin' a Missus Mary, d'Gran' Mammy o'de Higgs an' mo'. She teach' me 'bout lookin' aftuh d'house an' what d'awrduhly runnin' o'de fahrm got to be. Yuh know, sew up d'seams 'n' rips… 'bout keepin' thin's runnin' smoof through d'watuh like a well-'iled ship." Lucy describes Mary Higgs' tutelage, the grand matriarch figure, with decided fondness, when you consider the tedious tasks imposed upon her as a protégé, which often required quite the Herculean grip.

The complexity and maturity it takes to run a house in full order is not to be taken lightly rain or shine. Remember, Lucy was a young, audacious maiden's neophyte. Dexterity has inevitable, strenuous prerequisites that resourcefulness demands by degrees of time. Accustomed perfunctory, muscular acrobatics calls up an inimitable equanimity of endurance and mulls a necessary retainer to toe the line. God be praised in occupations of the greater good and invisible remedies that bind the ravages of time for a child of nine. Vile, vicissitudes warrant investigation, alright. Preying upon youth foregone, lost, or unsuitable, how do we not absorb or spew resentment's guile? Providence for Lucy pares ripe fruit in season and she, unquenchable for life, takes a juicy bite.

"I luhrn't d'sewin', meal cookin', what be gittin' mo' washin', when puhr season, an' how t'rem'dy a mis'ry's fevuh'd plight. At fuhrs' d'buttuh chuhrnin' 'n' coffee pawrchin' be so sawrly hahrd each time. It feel' like I's achin' from a fisticuffs fight. I takes t'cryin' 'n' whinin' 'n' snakes a res', when d'Missus be outta sight. Uhrly watuh fetchin', egg 'n' log gath'rin', fawrin' up d'kettle, an' cow milkin' be a tall san'wich o'cho'es goin' on day 'n' night. Lab'rin' from sunup wif no stop, 'til d'sun hit twilight. By day's en', I's soak't like a skuhrt jus' dip-dye', sweatin' from cain't see in d'mawrnin', 'til cain't see at night. Bleedin' blistuhs latuh, I gits t'knowin' d'lot. Lawd knows I tried. See, t'de Missus Mary, sweet, appuh pie orduh be d'mos' delightin', so I keep on a-tacklin' 'em, till dey's t'huh likin'."

"Now I gits on okay wif Massa Mawrcus' Gran' Mammy Mary, albeit d'pious schejuh bein' kinda tight. She aw'ight, ain't too snappish an' awll, ev'n teach me t'soot-clean muh teef an' dat be nice. At bes' I be back wif d'fam'ly kind. I gits d'opawrtun'ty t'atten' chuhrch too, t'anks be t'God aw'ight. Wuhrkin' dis a-way I s'pose 'bout six o'sev'n yeahrs passin'. S'pose I's mos'ly keen on 'ceptin' dis heah d'way thin's gon' be till I die."

Lucy's complexion radiates dear. She retells her days attending church like a cheery, exotic adventure across a fragrant frontier. Her interest in religion sparked vibrantly clear and begged my scrutiny to draw near. I enter a diary's side note scrawling, "I am audience to an actor's opening from a boxed-seat tier."

"Fav'rite time in awll dose yeahrs gotta be... goin' t'chuhrch! On D'Lawd's Day, all d'white folks be clam'rin' onta d'wagon wif d'bes' equippin' mares. Missus Prud'nce sho ain't suffuh a complimen' fo' airs cuhrlin' up huh buhrnt ches'nut hairs. She take' t'matchin' a pahr'sol 'n' bonnet t'each frilly frock she gonna wear. Der she go sittin' up high on huh cushion't chair. Bloomin' purty as a jus' picked spring posy she gonna presen' like a weddin' walk o'beauty down d'aisle a-pair. Yuh know dem spankin' new ships spawrtin' a whittl't stachuh, starin' out t'sea, blazin' a lady fair? Like dat I reckon. Cawrse, awll d'slaves ain't gonna go fo' sich trappin's o'needin' t'put on 'rageous airs... Maybe dey wash 'n' clean up some, if'n dey's lucky t'haf d'time an' lye soap ain't scarce."

"'Hind d'white folks on d'Sabbef' Day awll d'slaves be trailin' like pahrt o'de parade fo' some hol'day show. Cawrse d'Higgs fam'ly be in d'front o'dat float in d'coach, (Missus Prud'nce nachuhly bein' d'queen, fo' sho). I don' pay no mind on d'miles t'go. T'ank d'Good Lawd least ways fo' mighty muhrcy away from a-toilin' load. Strollin' on, I use'ly takes t'watchin' d'clouds cuhrlin' t'billuh 'n' roll. Sometime' dey's a-loomin' 'bove astretchin' like a cahrd o'pull't cotton on a blue blanket flo'. Othuh days d'clouds pass 'bove on a mount'n o'God's shuguh can'y floss 'n' piles o'snow. Dey be d'whippin' cream o'glawry fill jus' so." Invigorate across the changeable sky Lucy awes to a respectable glow.

"'Bout two mile' o'mo' eas' o'Grays Creek tow'rd Toone be d'whitewash chuhrch o'Eb'neezuh Ba'tis' wif d'bell in d'steepuh swingin' fo' awll t'see. I still sees d'cross too afah off an' heah dat bell clangin' cleahr 'n' free. Awll d'white folks clamuhr t'congr'gate in t'purty pews fo' greetin's b'fo' dey settlle in d'seats. Awll d'slaves stan' like a flock o'crows gawkin' in d'back... call't d'gal'ry packed in like a tin o'sahrdines." Lucy squeezes her arms at her sides and sucks in the sides of her mouth for a fish-face to signify a squished sardine. Her deep brown eyes, big as saucers, bug out wide as she stretches her neck forward as a gawker might be seen.

"Now I ain't claimin' t'unduhrstan' awll dat preachuh man say' mos' days. He belluhs, raisin' up d'Bibuh in sich a way, 'God make us all in His image,' he say." Lucy raised her right hand above her head, shaking an invisible Bible to a congregation. "I's gittin' confuse' an' commence t'conjuhrin' in muh head on dat fate, but I be a-lis'nin', a-singin', an' a-prayin' jus' d'same. I feel a-wonduh, a *mighty* wonduh in muh brain. Why's God make some folks cuhluhr't an' some folks so light an' some folks b'twix' d'two cuhluhs in play? If'n we's awll like Him, why's we awll lookin' differ'nt, each in dey own speshuh way, but I dinna say it. I behave."

"Den he say, 'God make each fo' dey own puhrpose', so I gits t'scratchin' muh head t'figguh cleahr. What be *mah* puhrpose heah? Maybe I's gonna care fo' d'white folk fo' muh puhrpose... I look t'de flo' an' furruh muh brow confuse' 'n' uncleahr. Den he say, 'Feah an' wait on d'Lawd'. Okay den, so... dat be what I be tes'uhfying t'do fo' d'time bein' heah.—Sho nuff don' haf t'wait long. D'Lawd done toll a 'nothuh chuhrch-chimin' bell o'dest'ny in d'nex' fo' o'five yeahrs.

PORTAL'S REPOSE

Just before the ebony drape of night's final curtain reverts, dreams dissolve from a filmy, faded picture. Visible sienna-tanned shadows, a sorrel stranger, stayed mottled in a tin-type vignette; and whet, like watershed adumbration, stick on the canvas of her mind, but a-blur. Dawn's fingers massage ration and reason to the fore and slumbering consciousness stirs. Climbing from her dreamy cavern colored in the comatose complexion of a deep sleeper, Lucy gives a dry, softly sucked-in gurgle, not quite ready for reality's arm-pinching return. She complies to the stanchion sergeant of the hall, a paternal clock who reprimands with speechless, soldiering ticks to be "up 'n' at 'em" at her.

Calloused knuckles buckle across rounded, sluggish eyes scrunching up the bridge of her nose with a vertical, crinkling mark. Lucy scratches at itchy, linsey-woolsey on the back of her winter garment, rubbing to the pace of a perceptive heart. Coldness bathes her skin with prickly shiver-bumps from the start. Drowsy fingers go fumbling and claw down to pull up a quilt Prudence's grandmother had tossed as a discard. She sat up clutching a consoling patchwork tightly and wishes the frigid air would be seized or, albeit ever so skimpy, the coverlet would grant mercy and give ward. Meagerly shrouding her shoulders as a tattered shawl, she closely clasps to her breast the cloth's thinning parts. Like a miniature muff curled up over her fists Lucy hugs the cover closer, up to her lips, and breathes longer, hot breaths, panting onto her fingertips in hopes of heating her cold-nipped body parts, but it feigns any real warmth. A stunted, widening yawn becomes barred from sound, when squelched by the aid of a flimsy, hand-me-down shard.

Dawn's fiery chariot fastens rays across the edifice with gleaming winks. Insurrection's muted moan relinquishes her ultimately, ode to the exhaustive routine on the brink. Still a young girl, the scolding clock's stringent, tyrannical tick pricks her ears to be up 'n' at 'em again. Not yet a maid, Lucy squirms on top of the straw ticking sparingly spent. Nightly the pallet badgers her back through its thickly slatted imprints. Breath ceases for a blink to ease wooden, trundle rollers invisibly back beneath the grandeur of the larger, loftier bed without a disrupting din.

"Tarry not, lest idleness be led." She heard in her head something Missus Mary always said. Nigh dog-tired, fidgeting to wrench her feet into the size-too-small, brass-ended brogans, a toe-squeezing challenge. All-encompassing moonlight fleeces the Massa's hall, hindering Lucy with heightened shadows, which leap off parapets. She bumps along hurriedly and pathetic, appearing more like the drunken fiddler stumbling home to bed at dawn after Friday night's shindig, zigzag fashion. Blindly groping, she frees a coarse, calico dress from the hook and mismanages a quick yank on the sack-like shape over her head. Left-angled darting accidentally rips a seam on the hem. A task to sew that later is added in her head before the tear grows immense. To pull string-ties together she maneuvers sideways and snags a sneaky peek over her right shoulder at the elderly Missus Higgs, encroaching worthy peace with jarring wheezes. Incoherent snoring echoes, similar to a runt pig racing, when chased past the barn and around the pen.

"Gathuh ginguh root, b'ile it an' add a few draps o'blackstrap m'lasses fo' some healin', t'roat cleahin' tea fo' d'Missus d'rec'ly." She added another mental note to her daily list right from the start.

Lucy wasn't a trained nurse by any means, but a whole country full of folk practice digging up roots and drying herbs to manufacture cures for healing or other medicinal fare. If anyone was sick or enfeebling, friends, neighbors and slaves all took turns to aid with the care. That was the way of it in those days. Folks most often take care of yours, if you take care of theirs. Leastwise, a touch of comfort and assistance was shared for common calamities to the best of your knowing and resourceful spares. Heaven forsake, a reversal of circumstance finds you or your kin with insufficient coffers clutching and a-begging for mercy or kindness repaid. In that case it persuades amenable people in the direction to be generally sympathetic upon nurse able rapprochement without delay. .

Roustabout to set sail, she mimics under her breath what Higg's offspring, often mockingly, regale, "She' gonna out-live de lotta us. Dat be fo' sho," Lucy smirks and goes about her business without restraint.

The ruffles of the loose-fitting kerchief garnishing Missus Higgs' emaciated, lily-white locks shuttle like oscillating corn-ear tassels and broadcast each liberating exhale blown. Cotton dimity with a crocheted edge hangs like blue cornflower silk, draping to the floor. They melt melodramatic like warm wax dripping down her carefully carved, canopy posts. Over the yoke of Missus Mary's elderly-white gown are fully starched sleeves flopped out in funerary fold. They float like an apparition within the berry-dyed linens, half-mast sails billowing in tow. Turning on tip-toe, sidling betwixt a door ajar and the frame, she feels along the wall and finds her way unseen, unnoticed. Waiting patiently are the ever imperturable panes of her special window. As an older teen she inhales deeply and magnifies the hold, anticipation of a private peace she calls her own.

Lucy instructs from her heart. "Take a-listen heah, muh Mammy gotta healin' art. Huh gift keep us from gittin' sick wif b'iled down May-appuh roots 'n' sich she make inta healin' med'cine, 'sides, gittin' t'see a doctuh be like findin' black truffuhs in d'duhrt roun' dese pah-rts. When folks be huhrt, ailin' o'suffrin', we use lots o'differ'nt flowuhs, roots, an' plants fo' rag po'tice strips, soakin' 'em in a b'ilin' tea an' placin' on d'skin wahrm. Dat be d'way o'thin's in dose days, y'awll pass along yuh ahrt. God bless Mammy dat, a clevuh soul fo' luhrnin' me from d'stahrt. Wuhrk' like a chahrm."

I see a smile, but it vanishes, unmistakable in the wake. An appeasing stint could hide a hay pile of memories poking like a rake. A spirit of disquiet is bereft in the beacon shining light from the face of motherly pride and praise. I suppose a judgment can be made for inexcusable, blanching ignorance that accumulates in the sea of waning human grace. Slavery's reckless fate notwithstanding, ripped years out of place. She knows she'll never again see her mother's smiling face.

"Res' in Peace, Mammy," Lucy ministers with an irreverent dip of her chin. "D'Lawd, He goin' t'bless us an' keep us free from hahrm." Her mammy had taught her to pray away from the ears of the 'massas'. "Grace 'n' muhrcy light d'way. Good mawrnin' Makuh o'de New Day", she whispered, "Amen."

The glass portal, precious to the day's events does not disappoint the heart. Welcome are resplendent surprises, popping spring-green buds, which punch out along the scraggly dangling twigs and bare willowy bark. Little leaves with a perfect pip of God's finger growing them into an ever greening spark. The initial brush strokes of a Seurat, pointillism painting beckons new beginnings, amorous adventures, and unknown opportunities after winter's buttoned up hibernation and takes flight like spring's first monarch.

"I see you puts on a purty green dress t'day."

She skips merrily to the serpentine stream subtly energized by Spirit and flirts with the forest foliage. Kneeling and reaching out to skim the pail Lucy fills it with the swashing solace of a cool, simmering splash. Carefully she sets the pail on a grassy clump, smooths and re-plaits her hair, then ties it up under her dusty-blue, cotton kerchief, the ends now ragged and frayed. Lucy peers at a spunky youth in the rippling reflection on display. Indeed, she smiles; there is brightness to opening the day.

Awash of the naked morn, the adolescent generously charges the water with a chill and flings it high.

Across her face the sensation of eye-opening experiences triggers a freeing sigh. Plumped, watery beads ply languishing fat, dewy drops upon her cheeks and produce a suitable, rubicund dye. Lucy deliberately ladles another brimming handful to imbibe. Wetness cascades translucent rivulets leaking out her lips, in shiny channels on her chin, and casually continuing down her wrists from tiny caverns between her cupped palms, and then down, soaking her front to sides. A good deal knurled in ribbons from a supping disturbance, the surface shell now blurs too dim for divining. The flux soon subsides to a mirrored silvery sheen, while she seeks shelter upward and gracefully arches her neck like a young black swan to address the infinite sidereal mantle of a closing night. The glories of nature bring inspiration to her sentimental soul, which grows in a depth of intelligence toward the savvy and endlessly resourceful type, optimistic despite her plight.

Embrace of heaven's hood with arms spread wide is part of greeting dawn in ritualistic stride. Lucy's left toe points down in a curtsy as the fraying edge of her hem is felicitously held to the side. She skips mildly and tops it off with a twirling pirouette of some kind. She feels spiritually unshackled like King David, dancing in joyous, biblical pride. Hers however, is to the sporadic hum of a country waltz she'd heard at the County fair one time. Pretend silk scarves with sleigh bells jingling are fluttering from her fingers, a fancy style she'd her the peddler tell tall tales about, a prince from some far away isle, except no one, towit God and His angels, are in sight. The window's repose always inspires with the tickling delight of breathable freedom brought to the forefront of her mind.

PRODIGIOUS
PONDERING

Verily, her visage fixes orientation on a chiefly, tranquil star toward the morning's north. Devoutly pious patterns of diadems and prisms would draw her daily to venture above and beyond the farm's woodsy back door. Lucy leisurely navigates her fingers, mid and fore, walking them through the air along celestial stepping stones, the circuit within the glimmering Drinking Gourd. Pensive unto consternation, she's poised a prolonged piece from awaiting chores, distinguished atop a majestic gem eternally forged. She points a petite index finger and pauses, further extending query of common folklore "Wuhr dey slaves t'de heav'ns agin dere might? Did dey escape from d'day t' be shackl't agin cryin' teahs dat drap as a-polishin' shine? Why dey ablinkin' like t'be watchin' back ev'r' night? Maybe stahrs is like de Queen o'Sheba wif a cohrt, all cavawrtin' 'n' dancin' fo' d'joy o'Jesus, high 'n' bright?"

Lucy, unbeknownst, summoned my youth as talks of innocence might. A fleeting, happier memory steals freely across my mind of diamond-shaped kites flying in Central Park, during a traditional, Saturday picnic rite. Upon release they take to the sky as birds with beribboned, multi-colored plumage tracing circles as they climb. I realize now that I was certain at one time in life, long ago, of Heaven's power to guide insoluble with wondrous insight, exposed in childhood's guileless delight.

"What be Yo' puhrpose fo' me in dis place?" She whispers inquiry to God as if close to His face, while tilting her head to one side like an anxious pup awaiting outstretched arms and a loquacious, encouraging phrase. Favoring forward to a knitted brow and scrutinizing gaze. Impassable shadows fade and pirouette enigmatically through the dim sheath, a primal barrier of trunks amid a sea of dense vegetation, pondering greatly.

"Whar dey hidin' in d'wilds t'keep safe? How dem slaves s'pose' t'eat an' make a way wif no money o'massa's lan' t'cult'vate?"

Silently a notion comes to Lucy, what if slaves *never* were freed like she'd heard one say, before he was chained and taken away… back to his brethren enclave… twas the life of shackled knaves. Her natural nonchalance marked haste sashaying back to behave. Cooking to the fire, bubbling as a fine kettle of black-eyed peas and chunky pork with a side of steaming cornpones, all homemade, Lucy dares not dally or delay. The double dose of tasks resumes resolve as the ebb and flow of a wave, charting her vigorous youth a teen's age. Ardor of a veteran servant-leader, chief cook, and bottle washer prevail with ambitions toward powerful purpose in favor with grace.

❦

On the beaten boards of the porch she gives an apple slice a nip and sips her tea with a hint of mint. Nostalgic wetness sits slick upon her lip and shines, when she lets out the merest giggle.

"I 'membuhs strugglin' dem fuhs' awk'rd buckets 'cross d'duhrt, 'cause I be too rangy, weakly as a littuh's runt pup, t'carry 'em hawswahrd boun'. Sloshin' 'n' stainin' d'groun' as much as gits t'de kichun pot, so's I makes mo' trips t'git d'nece'sry amoun'. Pavin' muh pafway up 'n' backs I be piddlin', evuh-which-way t'be foun'. Weeks 'n' weeks move on, whilst I scrub, lug 'n' pahrch t'beat d'ban' b'fo' I's pahr t'de task. Thanks go' t'God, muh body 'venchully change saucein' t'stren'th an' hahrdnin skin b'gin to fawrm awll 'roun' d'palm' o'muh han's."

Tenacious and audacious, never known to be a fool, long-suffering to labors too, she endures enterprising errands from the Missus' list of incessant toiling—that often seem the rule. The little one transfers 40 pounds of water from a bighted shore to the sorely blighted trough for the thirsty animal crew. Then, situating her "bony behind" on a shaky, three-legged stool, she sets to milking the mooing, bleaguered cows with a coo-some duo. A dulcet lullaby coaxes their cautious grousing and calms their fears, so Lucy continues to croon. Rubbing her palms in a frictional fury warms the fingers for squeezing udders as folks not immune to cold hands aptly do. It is a Herculean test to lift sloshing buckets of lukewarm milk table due. She blurts unliberated, guttural grunts under her breath to assist the muscles in stretching and bending as greener-growing boughs can do. Diurnal practice grooms her for self-reliance, until none is jostled from routing about the barn and round the chicken coop.

Squawking poultry stuff and plump as she scatters grain to fattened game. Lucy slings a small puncheon forward and aft in under-arching, childish sways to bash drudgery's load at bay. Reeds from the creek woven in a horn aplenty shape are hoisted atop a nest on the hen house gate. Acquiring eggs at a quickened gait, she works as if her heart is in every chore Missus Mary decidedly makes.

You can almost hear her overoptimistic and vivacious attitude sing out in her tasks, adding weight to the reason why she doesn't hear a stranger moseying around the corner just about now. Lucy pampers each precious oval as a newborn babe to the basket's bed. Attentively a-buzz with duties entrusted to the chief house maid, she is fully occupied, inspecting each egg for an excellent grade. The only thing on her mind is the next chore on her mental checklist: Put the dough kneaded in dawn hours on to bake.

━━╱╲╲━━

In 1898 means of flour were less tolerable, but were added to oil and yeast and kneaded together on the counter of her little cottage kitchen in New Albany's predawn inkiness, rewards of free intention at last. Towel-wrapped dough rests and farms a plain-edged tin hedging the small sill above an overcast iron, (clean as a slim, penny whistle) porcelain sink basin. A cursory glance at the chubby the mound grants enough reviewing inspection for a visual pass. Sniffing the tender rising bundle allowed aromatic assessment, so Lucy patted the homemade loaf like an infant just fed pap, burped its backside, and shed the turbaned wrap with a single, slightly damp towel slap.

A doughy center is impeccably cut to create a valley for the buttered gap. The creaky, oven door closes with a severe metal-on-metal 'BAP'. While we wait and sit, I notice Lucy freely folds perseverating creases with her agile fingers to flatten a hand towel and cap dignified dents across the cloth on her lap. She gives the towel a final creasing line and opens the heavy door quite fast. The steamy smell of fresh baked bread drifts into the house in a tantalizing waft. No pocketwatch necessary, when timing her craft.

ROOSTER IN
THE HEN HOUSE

By '58 the master's sister, Missus Prudence Higgs, sat in a puffed up parlor chair with cabriole legs waiting like a princess with her perfectly oval face. Her lips bow pink in that permanently pouting heart-shape below her smallish, upturned nose within a creamy complexion, white as a dusty miller, and surrounded by temple-spiraling corkscrews of shiny, dark cedar curls like a frame and fall down her back in bouncy waves. Prudence has a new slave, Cal, purchased from a big auction south a ways. Marcus Higgs, her brother, hired him to clean and mend the chicken coop, as well as a dozen other duties to hammer, pound, and put a plantation straight. No fault carpentry services are hawked forcible by slaves and sellers alike on the bidding platform, high in demand to any frontier's populace.

To beat the heat of the day he attends early and whisks his woolly head around the opening of the coop past the corner of the corn crib to assess any deterioration with an initial estimation visit. Suddenly a sweeter sight sways him from repairman to swain right quick. Cal marvels at the unexpected. He anticipates a winning stay from his newly stationed estate, but now fair fate delivers a fetching female to begin it. Consideration to the quarry, maybe love at first sight sends emotions flying off to an enchanted. A man like him is quickly persuaded by a gal like Lucy, still innocent, svelte, and feminine. The interest could not contain Cal's growing grin. Enterprising as he is, he chooses to swell a pause at the narrow rectangular entrance, which incidentally serves as an intersection against exit. He remains at the doorway pleased as punch to peruse a-pinin'. Lucy, full throttle faithful to chores and chickens, turns directly around to see him.

"Good mawrnin' purty lady dere. Don' be a bob-tail scare't." The stranger sallies in half-hearted, humor, satiating a fearful ear. "I come on t'mend 'n' clean d'coop an' wuhrk 'roun' heah. Y'awll can cawll me Cal. I be raise' due eas' by a Souf Car'liny pier. Please t'make yuhr 'quain'nce lil del'cate deer."

He regroups by addressing fast and jocund-busting bright, but that just adds emotion to the situation's shearing and friendly wit. Not knowing what to do she is taken aback, terrified, and touched to the quick. A sultry tone in his voice encircles her spirit though, so she does something she has not yet done to a man, afore to herein,—Lucy looks him in the eye somewhat spooked, which sends her doe-eyed heart fawning to a rapid pit-a-pat within.

To her admonition he cut a swell cloth in countenance, dark and handsome, tall as a blue-mountain pine touching heaven. (Lucy points from the porch to the raftered ceiling therein and touches upon her heart again.) A grand copy of Cal's grin grew on her face from what it must have been. She reaches out her hands to curtsy or shake his hand and say her name, but that confused her on which way to bend.

"Lu—SPLAT! Dem eggs tumbuh wif muh fraguh dispuhsition an' mo'! Sweet Lawd," (She slaps her hands at her thighs lightly and whips them down to the side, still wiping embarrassment away with the past, plastered with scrambled eggs, while shaking her head incontestable with hard no.) "D'basket folluhs, disconsuhrtin' d'scawre, an' catypult' some hens, still a-flappin', willy-nilly, an' flinchin' in a flust'rin' show. I be hot-cross buns blushin' by den, doncha know? Secr'tly though, I be beggin' muhrcy 'bove from d'Awlmighty Lawd, but I hang muh head an' peek up wif muh face glue' t'de flo'."

Torn slivers of dawn's splendid rays splay out in sparkling magenta behind his larger, blacker brand. Exterior to the sides of his darker shadow, a pale horizon ridge separates the jagged texture of rugged piked edges and progressively smokier layers of goose-down grays and Tuscan tans. Lucy wasn't sure if he was a prowler or an angel sent from above, but she couldn't take command of her voice to speak and stood, stock-still in silent recant. No egress at hand, but Cal's disconcerting reprimand. Albeit a damsel in distress she transformed in the last ten years from duckling to swan, buxom and beautiful on demand, even in lieu of the egg-covered mess she has to withstand.

With a smile ear to ear Cal hesitates at the door for how to help and then reaches out his hand. Not heard amidst the frizzled, chicken-balking din, he busts out in a deep, belly laugh positively grand. Worldly adroit and decent to a fault, he forms a doubly-strengthened man, just as much as she is petite and poignant in her shapely, statuesque stance. Besotted love birds hatch. Lucy sinks into a smitten-type creature, feminine without effrontery or admittance, just plain snatched. Heaven's meeting is a match consecrated quintessential, and so, meant to be tenderly attached.

Cal and Lucy have respectful terms with affectionate intentions from up and at 'em, reciprocated without demand. Endearing every day of the week and twice on Sundays, they share pleasant rendezvous, loyal to the day they began. He wheedles romance and charm with a permanent powdering of paprika spices that mingle in the mouth in an irrepressible dance. An explosion equal to Fourth of July fireworks set off inside her, his witty repartee, so grand. She plays coquettish and alluring to his liking, an ash-baked yam, naturally sugary and belly soothing bland. They entwine like hot-buttered biscuits needed to sop up creamy, fried sausage gravy all over a plate, quite serendipitous and uncanny.

A slave's life being concededly shortened for courting in the situation at hand, thus is such, Cal makes powerful in his amorous approach, markedly like a Dapper Dan. Being so good with his hands, he persistently plucks a wild flower here, takes baskets or buckets there, and fashions leaves to resemble fans. To present little sentiments cuffed offhand and aim like a gentleman gambling on a prize-winning thoroughbred themes his courting slant. Attentive and fancy like an English Shepherd Dog, humbly genteel, yet governing to focus his stance. Lucy countermands inward promptings and to maintain innocence, even after being wooed by his silky bass and that deep-south variance. Sooner answered, rather than later, he gathers courage and requests from the Master her hand.

"Cal ain't like a dawdlin' duffuh o'de cahrpet baggin' man. Afta a season he take' a notion t'marry me an' axks d'Massa fo' muh han'." Lucy chirps in cheery glee, "I be happy as a singin', spring crick't hoppin' nigh fo' luck t'de lan'." She swiftly says, "I sho do!" enormously grand.

NONE PUT ASUNDER

There is something to be said for being gratefully wed, when a service centers on affairs of the heart. Cal busts out his best bib and jeans not filthy from the farm; sensibility always attires in simplicity, superbly stark. Lucy glows in a gingham garb, not high-falutin fancy, just un-torn and gathered at her waist by the yards. Custom intentionally replete with an old broom at their feet, raucous… hardly. There are no party-sparklers fashioned for the celebration, although laughter after did intensify through the night marked and warm.

They jump clasping hands joyous as the greenest, long-horned grasshoppers in a field full of sweet white corn. Befitting glory, they grin ear to ear and praise the Lord for their union in the clearing just beyond an acre of seeded wheat sprouts starting to peek above topsoil in the morn. Lucy sees Cal standing brave as a suitor in shining armor. He shares her values, the responsibility and security she hopes for in a man, someone you would sit side saddle with on a horse and handy to the manner, yet kindly and full in ardor.

Amorous gestures are accepted upon acreage with gusto, though no ring is bestowed, no new gown worn, neither a crowning veil of lace adorns. The wayward, wild maypop just plucked is tucked adorably behind one ear near the rush of crimson flush to her cheeks; captivating as a babe asleep, newly born. Presentation of an ample chest of woodsy cedar by kin has not been carved, neither sanded smoothly worn, nor stuffed with a trousseau for the bride's first eve and morn. Consider the wedding processional, hope's sinuous stride, it too is clipped and shorn for occasion to stand side by side—little more.

There under rustling triangular-shaped leaves of a birch bark-white, tender promises of loyalty are sworn. Lucy gifts Cal with a piece of material embroidered with a marvelous heart torn off of the small, quilting square from Mama Higgs' old coverlet and sewn by her own handiwork. That night she pulverizes and boils some mint leaves making a warm tea to share after they complete that day's chores.

"Missus Prud'nce 'lowed us t'have a speshuh weddin' night." The apples of Lucy's cheeks perk up in remembrance with a precious smile. Elation overwhelms like Christmas in July, when the master gives slaves a delectable feast of roast pork with a slice of wild, gooseberry pie and a sip of cider to toast gaity of the times …to Lucy it felt uncommonly fine.

"One o'de slaves from d'neighb'rin' way pick't up a-fiddlin' ahrt, so folks take t'dancin' at d'pahrty. Slaves 'n' fam'ly alike be kickin' up plenny o'dus' steppin' 'n' stompin' togethuh, which is pyuhrfyin' t'de hahrt."

Awake as a wife now feels so good every morn. Lucy marvels at the rear windows world with a heightened sense of her purpose and power for the Lord. She caters to Cal, glossing cordially while he whacks a wood cord. A whimsical wave waggles with his cheeky, two cents worth. She stands in her peanut gallery vestibule to his early show and prays for family harmony.

"Impress muh fam'ly safe from hahrm. T'ank yuh fo' ahr blessin's, Deahr Lawd." She prays for accord to cover them like comfort from overflowing, fresh-picked fruit to make elderberry cobbler and plenty left over in mason jars to stock the cellar.

Prudence Higgs and Albert L. Chairs, well-heeled abreast of local influence, share promises that year as well, a grotesquely, swanky affair to attest. Although quite picturesquely romantic for guests, the gorgeous bourgeoisie glean prestige from a wedding fete. From appearance of the bridal company, beribboned with bows, bouffant wigs and bewitching smiles, "Wedding March" plays loudly by a seasoned, string quartet. Capricious as a peacock in her vision to the manner born bred, Prudence suffers stylish elegance of a foppish extravagant end, no less for a costumed queen not courting a crown (like "The Emperor's New Clothes"), insatiable to impress. Significant countenance of behavior proves antithetical to a translation of Prudence, her given name, "practical, discreet, or cautious".

Albert dons a high, bright-white starched shirt, bow-tied at the neck. He sports tailored pants with a singular, pin stripe dressed down the side, nonetheless favoring all ordered garments have creases deeply pressed. Prudence is enrobed with wide sleeves on a decorative stroll. All too pricey lace trimmings inset and buttons embrace the silken gloves, which string up her wrist pretty as pearly caterpillars on a summer's rest. A green, organdy gown festooned with golden flowers, cinched at the waist and the best gossamer stockings are all shipped from London and transmitted to Toone by pony express.

The bodice's collar, covered in a creamy, white cotton chemise is bedecked with tiny florets. The ensemble becomes complete with Grandma Higgs', heirloom cameo at the neck. Her voluminous, skirted crinoline cage completely envelops with yawning petticoat yardage at no expense for the impulsively catered-to fest. They postured from the church to Gray's Creek atop a wagon ornately filigreed with lilacs and draping white swags, money needlessly spent. Albert contracted the bodacious rig, hired for rent.

After the delightful ceremony, an announcement, dinner was served for the reception. The feast included sumptuous, Bollinger champagne from France, a mouthwatering, cornbread-stuffed, roast duck and a fattened, juicy ham with a side of yams and fried aubergine. The dessert course without exception saw scrumptious, spice-filled apples, berry pies, and a cake encircled by a delectable, dried fruit and nut bread concoction. Lucy cooks feverishly throughout the previous evening for the occasion. Feasting fit for royals and rounds of toasts flood innumerable from multiple bottles uncorked for consumption. A might unctuous, but verily, speeches and a frivolity of dancing dalliance follow inebriation's expunged inhibitions. Entertainment for the evening ended as if to eclipse a military ball, closing with a fireworks exhibition.

Married and living by the Mississippi River, Lucy's last master is the oldest Higgs' heir. Unexpectedly he died from a fevered, snake bite scare, which leaves his wife, child and slaves in a bit of a snare. The young Willie

Higgs, subsequently, became the last surviving male heir. During that same season, not more than a blink after their betrothal is shared; Prudence and Albert secure the slaves and remaining portions of the plantation from here to there as swift as a raven could fly the papers legally prepared. **Now**, Lucy is considered the property of Prudence Higgs Chairs, so thusly, slave to Master Albert Chairs.

"Cawrse, d'sojuhs encampin' dat come t'rough Bol'vah fairgroun's, tuhrn't dat city cawrt hawse an' sich upside down, so dey's not much recawrdin' known b'fo' dat time t'be foun'. Guests went t'dat weddin' an' see'd awll dem sights 'n' soun's. Some try t'tes'ify dey not in d'law, till dey git der papuhrs agin afta de wahr done leave town. Wahrs is awful drea'fuh fo' all d'folks, no mattuh which side y'awll cawrtin' 'roun'. Ain't d'God o'Glawry put men from bof sides in d'groun'?"

"It happen' aw'ight. I swear, han' t'Bible, 'cause I bakes dat sweet cake fo' d'groom 'n' bride. I makes mos' dat feas' so fine. Fact o'de mattuh be, d'Massa hire't extr' slaves t'catuh t'guests dat time. Folks arrived by 'n' by from fahrms 'n' plantations neah 'n' wide. Kin come heah from souf Miss'sip' cleahr up 'n' down dat entahr rivuh, ship'n' line. Tabuhls be set amon'st d'strawng, fawll pines, spahrklin' canduhs, tawll 'n' white, an' flaw uhrs smellin' sweetes' o'roses, fresh from d'vine. I nevuh see'd a weddin' cel'brate' so gran' in awall muh life by dat time. D'Massa 'n' Missus Chairs' pahrty las' all day an' int' mos' d'nigh'. Guess dat' awll I gotta say 'bout dat shindig, 'ceptin' dey sho frame a pichuh o'hap'ness fo' der station in life."

BLESSINGS'
ABUNDANCE

Verbal consent settles the pair on a paltry parcel to work. Ambiguous in allowance, but quaintly compressed to indifference in one room, they hammer their hut with hearth. Gratitude given to Cal's crafting skill and Lucy's cozy perks. They create space primitive of order with a thin, rock-chimney to cook, heat, and romanticize, when they meet alone, a dwelling unhindered, home for what it's worth. They opt to pony-up yonder and build by Grays Creek, whereabouts the tan, sandier bottom surges. It's generously filled by an assemblage of the Good Lord's fresh fish as they meander from the larger body of water.

Circumjacent to the barn's easterly wall, their structure perches within view of the verdant forest. Various trees, thicker birches, blindingly tall to a blur, black tupeloes bursting with peduncled, greenish-white clusters and large limbed ironwoods arch skyward. Slim sycamores too, stately soar, then crest and clip edges in and around the creek's twenty acres. Their shanty keeps slim quarter, juxtaposed the corn crib, to withstand the weather's worst. This caps 'n' curtails divot chinks from outside elements, likely allowed as poltroon gales sidle surreptitiously and seep through shanty cracks come autumn's infirmities. The walls are now weatherized with a moist patch of mosses, gravel, and soot-mixed earth. Inside it's just tall enough to hang onions and herbs from rafters in winter, respectable on completion, morein, ceiling to ceiling, floor to floor, it holds a plum goodly girth. He takes time to gather flat stones for a drier floor, instead of dampened, desolate dirt.

They focus primarily on filling the abode with babes and toddlers, now that there's a place where they can grow unbesmirched in miraculous mirth. Their souls swell to overflowing as the cup in biblical lore, when a wink more than nine month's thence Lucy gives birth on a crystal, clear morn. They name their baby girl Mona, a blissful bundle of joy to bless their world. Old-time river songs echo in serenade through the shanty ceiling with merciful stores. Lullabies linger on high as innocence knocks on the door inviting love galore. The infant snores within Lucy's shoulder sling during daily chores. At night Cal scrapes wood to a whittler's beat as weary Mama Lu' pumps Mona's crate-box cradle with her feet on plank supports. Sufficiently sturdy, the crib proves just enough for a season of growth and a bit more. While softly singing "Rock Me to Sleep", encore upon encore, Mama Lucy cuddles Baby Mo' in joy to the Lord.

"I declare His heav'nly hahrmony' bulges plain like d'pyuhr vapuhs o'sweet, mount'n-scrub aftah weeks a no rain. Blessin's cannonade, effectin' greatly in d'basic way. God be lifted up in dat instan' a roly-poly babe come onta dis Erf. I know it' not d'en' o'wuhrkin'… o'many a mis'ried strife, but as God be muh witness b'fo' I goes t'muh grave, *I's nevuh goin' t'let dem sell dat chile o'glawry away.* I jus' breef it out t'de air, t'no one in puhrtic'luh, but t'Cal's heahrin' eahr, an' t'God, who knows all d'thoughts I holds deahr. It come out quiet-like, whisp'rin' an' sawrta bref'less wif a sol'tare teah on muh face."

"Savvy Cal tuhrn't t'me an' says, 'Listen heah. We b'longs t'God Lu', no man dat pay t'own us o'don' pay. 'Venchly we gonna go back His way. Mo's be ahrs fo' safe keepin' in d'time bein' an' we gonna do jus' dat, 'til we awll gits up t'Heav'n t'stay.' Praise d'Lawd fo' sendin' me Cal. He alluhs knew jus what t'say."

➤╱╲◄

At about nine the cat curled up tightly. Lucy lumbers to a stand with her cane, choosing to retire inside. A breath of bare necessity inside, the sitting room wields a tiny table between two wingbacks angled informally, when conversation ebbs at low-tide. They distribute similar, cloth decoration headrests in small stride. Nifty, needle point samplers I espy privately signify pillow-talk, mottos clearly defined. 'Home sweet Home' and 'God is Good' must have been a wedding surprise, when she married John Nichols in '69. Distinctions of character can indeed dignify nominal pride.

"God don' stop wuhrkin' yuh know," she said a little louder. "No mattuh what folks be doin' in spite o'der own free will agin one t'nothuh. He ain't done His wuhrk s'pawrly dat His folks don' know, when it's done right. Praise t'Jesus fo' puhseverin', so's we know how t'try. Praise Him too fo' d'babes, 'cause dey's so precious in His sight." Lucy chimes in from the next room about the simple pleasure of breaking bread, sandwiched between a scrap-book of her life. On minor unmatched plates, crunchy crescents of peeled, jade-green, granny apples sidle up to two steamy bread slices.

"Well, fo' a time o'fo' t'five yeahrs ahr days be bright like to a newly, mint penny. We's full in love like celabratin' a Jub'lee... 'Cawrse, nothin' stay d'same wuhrkin' fo' d'greatuh good o'de Lawd, don't yuh see. I ain't t'know it at d'time what twista be brewin', soon t'flare rife wif puhr'lous pain smack dap inta d'smiddy's hottes', pyuhrfyin' flame, but der be a great change a-comin' dat gonna crippuh dis country"

Late one night in war's reprehensible year, the full moon glows with bloody rings, dire and ominous, like the eyes of a rabid dog, intimidating in angry reds. Looming larger than life the lunar clouds carried a caustic, rebellious threat. Lucy saw them before stabbing as piercing rays through the cramped cabin's scaffolding like a charge of bayonets. Howling like wild wolves, prowling their prey's scent, hideous winds of a vociferous nature often preempt thundering, Tennessee torrents. Their shanty structure was simply unfit for storms so intense.

Differing doctrine is cast inside nonetheless. A tranquil scene encases the family trio as a well-made, wool mitten. They sleep as spoons nesting. The protective fealty provides fidelity and encases them, ethereal and lambent, but her motherly declaration still hangs in the air and rises in Almighty assent. Lucy unknowingly prayed a condensing, veiled message compelling the angels of Providence.

SOUTHERN SQUALL

"Thank d'Lawd fo' life an' mo'. Three yeahrs be whiz-zin' by like a steam locomot', maybe fo'. Mona be machuhrin', sho as rivuh, cat tails grow. Cawrse, jus' as we gits t'de summi' o'de rewahrds o'life, a change gonna roll t'test yo' faith lil mo'. I's a-runnin' d'big haw-shol'. Cal came t'runnin' d'othuh pahrts o'de fahrm in a sim'lar station, when des'ny go an' thrash a lightn'n bolt cross awlready plowed 'n' seed' rows. In decades pas' I nevuh cross'd'boun'ry o'Massa's fahrm fo' wuhrk o'show. I'se mo' like a huhrmit, 'ceptin' fo' outin's t'chuhrch wif d'folks. Now Cal, he go out oft'n, hire't t'Bol'vah an' trollin' woods fo' sq'ruhls, quails, rabbits 'n' wild hogs 'n' sich wif his huntin' ahrm on d'go."

"One day in d'muggies' Mawrch on recuhrd, I spies 'im through d'back kitchen winduh wif a severely stud-yin' look t'his face… It be a look I well know. His eyes be shiftin' 'n' dahrtin', ahrms set akimbo. Now I ain't one to beg troubuh no mo' o'intr'ducin' folks t'a sorry sho', but I makes like I needs a few eggs mo'. Dis heah gal, know huhr man like a man know his hawrse fo' sho'. He got sumpin up his sleeve, but don' want no ones t'know. D'rec'ly tow'rd d'chicken coop, I trots like a hawrse on propuh show dat know jus' whar t'go.

We hit d'spot sacr'd t'ahr hahrts. Cal yank us t'a squat like we's pahrt o'some prankish sneak on a lahrk. I be lis'nin' keen as I can an' looks t'his pow'fuh, bahrk-brown eyes so rightly smahrt. He be spout'n' 'n' sput'rin' fastuh dan a rogue, skit'rin' skir'l, but he ain't got time 'nuff t'tawk d'pahrt."

By 1860 American economy had become brutally off-kilter, but slave states were allowed a continued show. Conversely, industrialists of the north didn't have slaves minding the majority of the workload, if at all, and stuffed their displeasure, until it was like a cannon bloated with a keg of gunpowder set sky-high to implode. A tragic thread unravels and the tearing tapestry of politics and parsimony preside heavily over each household. Labor's champions hope for a dose of humanty in the corner of slavery's abolishment, but a pound of cure did not atone. Those opposing dispose an attitude of entitlement, more akin to greed or an apathy that grows. Deconstructed, the fabric of our nation's interpositioned flag hangs low and coldly flown.

Man engaging man stratifies the pasturage of blood that begins to flow, a fight looming larger than the gallows' poll. Unremitting battles comingle in fields, red as wine and burned as black toast, until the dead outnumber any gain from victory's toll. Farther than the frontier advances the stretch of dead erodes families and souls. It suffers no exception to color, credo, your brother's breeding, broken down shanty on a squatter's shy or plantation with hundreds of acreage to boast.

"'D'fawres' be crawlin' wif men not shy t'shoot an' slaves aplen'y ' scapin' nawrthuhly fahr. Dey's scoutin' 'n' fawr'gin'; sizin' up fahrms on dey own shrif' 'n' hook. I done muh own 'ves'gatin' an' see'd 'em congr'gatin' like a drea'fuh bahrriuh o'fists a-doublin' hahrd.' Like a feah-fuh win' rattlin' winduhs, Cal jabbuhs on from d'hahrt wif mo' dan a belly full t'repawrt. I's uncleahr an' beg d'whole mess t'git repeat from d'stahrt."

A thunderous, vitriolic, gray coat unfurls, hovering over turbid skies. It rapidly turns into blinding blanket of torrential sheets, further darkening the screen of night. Downpours deepen and accumulate tears of adversity by and by in mud-filled morasses, mired to the booted thighs. Wandering woods hold fast, vastly unhindered as God wills, but for a season in time. Southern slaves run and hide, fight or die. Thousands perch on the auspicious precipice apprised of freedom's promise for basic rights. With an upright heading, bedraggled, footsore and hungering they try escaping to northerly countrysides.

The poorly plead for liberation, not Liberia and pray assistance from Providence, not the government on high. Hope unleashes anew in life, incisive of the incubus campaign or possible rights. The pilgrimage of oppression pushes prerogatives like a people's flood on the rise; numbers keep increasing by the following July like uncut grasses spreading wide. Known and unknown fears from foes identified and nameless take sides. Prayer bowls full of human tears tip over belied and spill millions of prayers with an inconsolable, whimpering cry. Despondent droplets do not deter the ensuing issue of slavery in severity nor veer off to a valley to pool and subside.

"'Cleahr down t'de fairgroun' by Bol'vah, d'Union encamp'. Dat mil'tary gonna mustuh a-mess o'men from awll ovuh d'lan'. Dey be buildin' up suhr'ous ahrmies from whut I unduhrstan'. Some folk be sayin' dey enlistin' slaves an' heppin' 'em git t'freedom agins' d'law exhawrtin' contr'ban'.' Cal be rattlin' on wif gibb'rish, jit'ry like straight up chaw spit-kick't a tin can tahrgit. Muh blood be racin' 'roun' fastuh dan a houn' on a spring hunt fan d'fawres' fo' rabbits."

"He ain't stoppin' an' jabbuhs on, 'I be plannin' fiuhrce, muh Lu', strat'gizin' b'fo' we be sol' souf o'heah an' haf ahr fam'ly pull't apahrt wrong. D'heat 'n' fiahre be knockin' on ahr fron' dawr like junguh drums in a wahr song. Lawd knows we's not safe heah fo' long. B'fo' d'nex' moon, d'ahrmy gonna p'rade dis way in a full, wahr-mawrchin' throng. Mawrk muh wuhrd in d'Bible o'God's Grace, dis heah Union fight be whar we belong.' I be shocked like I's standin' in a light'nin' stawrm holdin' a coppuh rod."

"Cal go on wif his finguh straight up t'muh face, 'We ain't tethuh't t'de trunk like a beat' junk yahrd dawg left lone t'pace his fate.' He take t'puhrsuadin' like a bee abuzzin' right by muh eahr in a hushin', hahrt-racin' scare. I be thinkin' he goin' t'leave me an' Mona fo' a sec', so I jus' lookin' through space in a tizzy't stare an' sucks in touchin' muh han' t'muh hahrt gaspin' fo' air. He disclose 'nuff t'give me a fright. 'We's in nahways puttin' d'cahrt afo' d'hawrse, so don' you take t'quer'lous sighs. I be goin' t'keep muh eahr t'de groun' an' muh eaguh eye t'clock d'prey fahr 'n' neah. 'Mind yuh, we ain't mawrkin' nowhars t'nigh'. Yuh jus' keep lis'nin', Lu', on d'sly.'"

Disregarding harry-carry, Cal kindles a calm resolve in his eyes, kisses her forehead softly, and hurries out of sight.

"Lawd gotta have muhrcy on ahr souls. We'se goin' t'git sol' o'take t'de back roads wif a chile in tow."

Lucy denigrates to elect flippant, negatively and low, malady maligning courage of character, if truth be told.

Crisis can command quarrels with the nay-saying self, which if left therein, a cynical fashion is all too often bred. I, myself, have been a fretful victim to this virulent dread. Drama wrestles imbalance, unchecked thusly, it can unravel like the pull on a loose, derisive sweater thread. Without thinking first on brave plans for action, as needs to be led, any fears fed or unescorted and undone exculpate the ends for cavalier minds asleep on the job in un-battened beds, weighing wanton and running amuck instead. Even taking up residence for a swashbuckling spell, the serious enterprising of injurious thoughts can purport poison to dwell, drinking dregs from a cup convoluted with dread. Pray for guidance to stay the course from the Spirit for a clearer head.

"What goin't'be d'lessuh o'two evuhs only God know'?"

Serving sensibility toward the greater good is better off said. Responses spawned from the Providence positioned heart witness a higher path exsposed. Waiting on the Lord most accurately shows which road remains open and which should be closed, be them as they lay before you forked or opposed.

She dismisses herself, but spins on a fine spindle, scuttling an unsuspecting red-feathered hen's roost. Lucy's confidence to conceal rises and she gently cups an apprehended egg in hand, to rightly engender a ruse. Questions from her respite at the faithful rendezvous may now assume an answer of no ill repute or at least minimally confuse. Lucy shook her head and took perspective skyward, desperately due. Secretly supplicating Savior for the full armor of faith or in God's saving grace a surrendering truce... a hope not yet materialized as an optional queue. One last look-see in her window's repose shows Cal trot off into the woods out of view.

"Lawd keep muh fam'ly safe from hahrm an' bless us fo' Yo' puhrpose t'be used."

When in the throes of inevitable, forlorn events, as one hopes, the impenitent stain shall offenses expose. I cogitate the Heavens may allow the scales to remain off kilter long enough for the swiftest arrow to strain a bow just so. Injustice as well weighs greatly unto exemplified fruition before the oppressive trial God has let loose can come to a close. Time to off-put the glasses of tenets written and read, so colored in rose. Longitudinal as the Mason Dixon flows, a line plows at Fort Sumter's soil with seeds planted to explode. There is brother pent against brother in a contradictory relation seeing many a family's foundation swiftly erode.

The very establishment of our country crumbles into the sands of a shifting, sink hole. Unapologetic, a separation grows and pulls America, flailing arms, under an icy floe. Our grander purpose sinks beneath like a pernicious, leaky boat. Augmented volunteer calls continue, as an effete, political force of southern states harvest particular, political events and full on war unfolds. Woolen coats pop egregious seams with arrogance and stubborn greed, not for a greater moral goal, which butts powerful heads repeatedly and ruminates in a monstrous collide for dominance, until the whole, ghastly matter implodes.

Families must now claim sides, Union loyalist or Confederate rebel, armies initiate ever lambasting episodes. Battle upon battle begins to take men untimely to their heavenly home. Stacking graven as they lay cold, soldiers stampede like lemmings following a drummer, "the pied piper" to an unsuspecting sea below or possibly likened to an assailing avalanche, which suffocates men beneath deceivingly angry, bloody snow. It is a ubiquitous tragedy no matter which way you go.

Other folks, deserters and the like, stash themselves in trees, barns, cellars, wagonbeds and ditch grasses, when the visually constraining smoky backlashes fill the air during skirmishing clashes. Some folks fraught with contention conceal themselves countrywide to Canada, yielding to probability's chances. Still others, as the true number remains unknown, extirpate their families and familiar conditions to the sojourner's diasporic roam of daring, fortuitous dashes. These battles rage continuously north to south and east to west at economic and philosophic impasses. Meanwhile down in Natchez, Prudence Chairs took to reading about Mississippi mêlées to Albert and the younger Willie from *Harper's Weekly,* notwithstanding her yen for advertisements and fashion. (These men of means didn't see war, because they could pay for military replacements with cash.) Though they were allowed to sit back with their get-out-of-war passes, they were not missed in combat. The photographers continued to pop their blinding flashes. News headlines continued to report catastrophes, battles and skirmishing clashes with dramatic commentary printed in columns fat with exaggeration on the tail of notable facts.

DIVIDED
AGAINST ITSELF

Angst of information casts her character stem to stern and unrefined. Lucy gathers waning faith, paling in aesthetic confection, whilst watching clouds willfully collide. Lazily they ebb past her window's repose with a lofty bias, taking no political side. Distaste from life is invariably washed out, even in instant's observation, cleansed by the spiritual palette of the sky. Veritable oceans of crystalline understanding begin to abide and desire a longer swim, but she has to dip down from on high. Dire developments keen to angry arms rise up ineffably vexing in the fullness of hostilities, devastating victims at your door, and without introduction's asking, make themselves at home by stepping inside.

"Onions," Lucy affirms on the sly. The elucidation energizes a relieving, slowly blown sigh. Through pursed lips she whispers an additional item like a ventriloquist might, "Peppuh," pilfered for that night.

The contentment of the kitchen, consoling for nineteen years' time, still counsels comfort to chores compliant as if just another night. She continues cutting carrots and onions, swiftly pocketing bits by and by. Chopping speaks a relaxing rhythm undenied; the blade clicks a familiar droning pattern against the wooden slab with each slice of the knife. Lucy entertains a listening lean, careful to abide as the double edged blade can exact a fatal slice.

Conversation drones in the quiet of the drawing room's exquisite pride. Lucy served tea and went back to dinner's preparation, but the natter of the latter room suddenly lowers in register like brook water heading toward rapids, a menacing murmur of the clandestine kind. Her ears perk directionally, listening like a marmot stretching its shoulders and back to espy, the protective posture of a dangerous clime. Any slave lucky enough to work in the house secretly knows all within, whether they choose to tell or not what its residents may openly deny.

While the thumb and forefinger pinch the handle, Prudence's prissy pinky points up and out wide, while lowering a lavender floral patterned cup, delicately encircled with a gold band on white. The dainty, porcelain demitasse cup clinks on the saucer, when set tableside. Proper etiquette is never too far out of sight.

Three burly bootsteps move burdensome from the adjacent wingback chair toward the majestic, mirrored mantel of the dignified, stone hearth, ticking like a time bomb to the basest watchwords, "We'll sell the lot down south, if the price is right. Pack light. I'm off to Toone for supplies."

More than just a poor choice of words, Albert's articulation swears no affinity of kinship with her, her child, or her husband in what she has always admonished as an esteemed time. Renunciation of marriage seems more amenable than suggesting the selling of slaves or a southward flight. Point in fact, the discussion deems more bearably appropriate for the dog, a horse, or maybe the unfortunate toy of a child's delight. Thoughts suddenly distort and decay in a gulp, snagged mid-throat, and cause blood to pulse and throb in apoplectic fright... Lucy swallows hard, starts breathing shallow and wants to shrink and hide.

"You may keep Lucy, if you like." Ten overzealous strides march to the front door and ricochet inside. Reverberating, worldly perfidy wash over her like a tempestuous wave at high tide.

"Muh gut knot up like a Miss'sip', shipmate' rope. He done twis' thin's t'suit his se'fless soul. I heared ' nuff t'make muh blood b'ile, but felt muh han's growin' col' as if muh blood stop' flow. In ev'ry sense o'de wuhrd I's lost, but dey's no compass t'guide o'sun to show me d'way home. I be disb'lievin' d'Massa goin' t'make a move souf, 'til I heahs it wif muh own two eahs... like a jus' load' gun cock't slow' by head from a Wes' Vuhrginny, mount'n outlaw raisin' a ruckus as he go'. Muh brain begins t'discombob'late, dizzy, like I be knocked six by a bawrd on d'nose. I be waitin' fo' no man t'shuck off an' find Cal; see if'n he's in d'know." Lucy was traumatized, pregnable on the prospects of Mr. Chairs' promulgating post.

Regular attendance to tasks, tossing garden vegetables in with potatoes to slow boil in the kettle, readied a hot meal according to the Master's wile. Radically anomalous options sit atop her shoulders in solitary reflection like two ton weights from news of the morrow's sentencing crime. Feigning routine indifference, Lucy ruminates a tongue-tied while, although it hampered her happier style. Ripened rosemary sprigs and salt flavor the stew, but a few rotations finish the seasoning from the peppermill grind. Pepper pinches join the purloined onion slices already pocketed out of sight. She spanks her hands thrice in a perpendicular smack, well satisfied.

Missus Prudence's toddler is checked just as a nursemaid daily might, which includes looking in on Mona, when they play together each day at this time. She stands simmering at the door frame forcing a smile. The girls are having a romp with dolls inside. They pretend encircled by a protective perimeter of miniature, play furniture. Cal fashioned the set Christmas last, surprizing the little tykes. The innocent sight, oblivious to susceptibility, will verify nary a single day's fight. Surfacewise, dandy to fine, a propaganda poster for *Harper's Weekly* to advertise. Lucy took one look at sweet "Mo's" skin, darkly akin to the missus' child of ghostly white, insofar as she espied, the population's preponderance toward color aesthetic testified to a muddy line.

Something strikes a sudden chord all at once linking the whole shebang across the synapses of her life. A voice from the past, as if right nearby rang from inside her head, easily identified…Massa Chairs! He gave commentary on our president one night. Sickening and sanctimonious, the retort, 'Hillbilly to Yank-on-high, what hubbub and nonsense,' quite the reactive reply. Though first heard back near '59, it rang out clear and bright. Albert's character of ethics emanates fear like a fox run amok in the hen house thieving eggs before first light. "The Great Emancipator" who determines our vast country's fate suffers to his own prejudice and strife.

"A hawse in divide canno' stand." She evaluated the verse openly under her breath, hurriedly touring the grounds in search of Cal outside. Those words were initially dismissed years ago, but now specifically imply. This is the only home she's loved, nay stronger than brick and mortar, a familial bond she made and prayed for; and for which she would have died. She stands conflicted to flee or have the blessing of her womb denied. The memory of a scared little girl behind her mama's skirt trying to hide and waking in a wagon on the saddest day of her life flashes before Lucy's eyes. She closes them to the noises of her mind, realigns herself emotionally and mentally as a mother on the lam and begins to prepare for a new kind of life.

"*No one gonna sell dis sweet chile o'mine!* We gonna be fo'evuh a broke home now, on de rivuh's op'site sides, dividin' us fahr as a canyon d'Lawd stretches wide, a fam'ly pull't as de'cean tide t'tide." She contemplates on the comparative contrast of Lincoln's loving, worldly wisdom and Albert's pejorative platitudes, so apathetic and snide.

"Ah," she gasps as drowning ideas come up for air! "Der be Cal!" He looks up and she motions with a negligible neck nod to meet at the chicken coop on the other side.

SALVATION
IS COMING

Lucy excuses herself to fill a kettle with water and rummage for tea in the kitchen cupboard as she has done in New Albany on many a day. I have to admit, taking intermission at this juncture leaves me at seat's edge, a quandry's vortex to contemplate. It is crystal clear from what I know of Lucy that she would never be swayed to betray, though, also an unlikely candidate to stay. I know she would not test fate to help Prudence with *her* babe, even if their offer included a nursemaid's *wage*.

Could she leave without Cal, bloodhounds chasing in a life threatening race? Would she leave as a lone wolf with her suckling cub, daring the hands of fate? Misunderstood, inscrutable acts accumulate in the belly like a dark draught drunk quickly to erase the dread, dankly opaque. Albeit discrepant correspondence disagreeable to an ear, the intriguing ripostes were not yet outward played. As I sit with a perponderance of possibilities, a hearty, euphonious hum hales. "Come Thou Fount of Every Blessing" beckons me melodious and blithely blissful from the kitchen as only a cappella can sway.

"I nevuh has a peck o'truhbuh 'memb'rin' dat fatefuh day. As God be muh witness, it sho 'nuff change' muh life evuh-which-a-way."

Vulnerable in visage, she looks straight at my face from her rocker, but leans toward me at the waist, more intimately grave. I try to readjust in my seat and chock up under the armrests, a captured, intimidated brace. Try as I might though, I couldn't unhitch from the intensity in her face.

"'Ceptin' dem cons'quences fo' muh chile be considuhbuh put t'mind, but handlin' dem 'spons'bil'ties, now dat be d'Lawd's cake t'bake. No time t'countuhbal'nce dearth, death, 'n' life, mus' toss dat at d'feet o'de cross on high. Lawd knows we be jus' as safe goin' souf as passin' any picket line. If'n it be d'Good Lawd's will, den we gonna git dere, if'n not, den His will be done jus' fine. Awlthough somewhar's down inside, I be wontin' t'fall t'muh knees weepin' inconsol'buh like a babes' blubbrin' cry. I tugs at muh bootstraps, 'cause dey's no othuh chawce fo' d'sake o'muh chile—but t'leave it awll b'hind."

"Muh lil maid, Mo', be in d'straw palle' on d'flo' dreamin', whils' I kneel t'pray as sombuh as de day. Oh, thank God fo' Faith! D'new moon priuh signuhfy time fo' new beginnin's, a clean black slate. I be fixin' t'tell d'Lawd we in His Awlmighty Han', soon's we leave dis heah estate. Cal be comin' wif a nod we's fixin' t'be on ahr way. Take t'knees I say, an' implo' d'Lawd fo' t rav'lin', anguh's muhrcy an' protectin' light's grace. We put on d'ahrmuh o'de Awlmighty to say, 'Amen' in Jesus' savin' name."

"I gits out d'onion 'n' peppuh stow't an' commences t'rub d'paws o'lil Mo'. Den, I rub muh feet 'n' hands b'fo' I pass it off t'Cal, so he can have a go. 'Keep dat,' he whispuh't low. 'I's t'head 'em off d'scent wif a preten' rodeo show an' meet y'awll neahr d'Hatchie fawrk down d'road. Der, we gonna cross t'gethuh whar d'watuh gots d'slowes' flow.' Sumpin' tell me t'grab d'small washin' tub an' a few pahrcels fo' whatevuh may come up yuh know. Cal take' great care wif Mo'. She' jus' sleepin' like a skir'l in d'wintuh's wood, cuhrl't up tight in a hibuhrnatin' hole. I sen's praise t'de Lawd she ain't goin' t'know right off 'bout dis heah changin' tale o'woe. I smoof an' kiss't huh head aftuh Cal scupp't huh up like a bag o'tatuhs. He whispuhs, 'I luvs y'awll head t'toe.' We's good t'go."

The trio rises quietly, when plantation lights douse for evening repose. They cross the large sward into the heavy, humid air of summer's swelter as fear's feverish excitement intensifies, producing perspiration's sweaty glow. Cal's heart is pounding loudly in his ears, but Lucy doesn't realize, because her's is pounding too. With Mona slumbering on Cal's indomitable shoulder they sneak off to the outhouse as their first excuse. Opening and closing the privy, so none suspect as one naturally, nightly removes. If they are stopped they will say Mona is ailing, a primary alibi to elude. Intrigue now tested travailing and true.

A second act secures perspicuity, aspiring to confuse. The night's velvet curtain rises and reveals a backdrop for the scene, a veiling bamboozle. Grays Creek adds bilateral opposition, so they choose to cross for a subtle smoke and mirror subterfuge. Mona saddles daddy's back and clutches onto his neck, a snuggling papoose. Cal and his precious package dangerously dovetail the stream. Mona's still snoozing. They disappear undisclosed on an eastward trek through the cold water, which creeps thigh high to carry out the ruse.

Rudimentary calumny of his scent residue traipses through the forest and remains etched on the plants and trees in tiny grooves. Lord forbid, it suffers insufficient in extent, if Master Albert's dogs trammel loose. Blood-heated hounds may snort any struggling hunt trails, when their bustling, baited breath pursues. Evildoers make a living off contraband's reward, which pays through the nose, if masters so choose. As soon as he reaches the willing, verdant woods, he doubles back to Hatchie's fork like smoke up a flue. Under a bleak and balmy moon numerous avenues of approach may amicably be put to use.

She watches them evaporate like the mountain's morning mist and a knot of desperation in Lucy's stomach ties itself to the pitchy blackness, decorated with dismay. Skillfully adjusting to the tricky terrain, dodging and snaking toward freedom, Cal seems to easily adapt without insecurities' mistakes. Mysterious buttonwood beams bolster horizontal columns of cloudless, leafy sprays and distract Lucy with elusive, silvery, eggplant-purple light, at play in pin-thin rays. They flush past and between the bent, low-slung branches and overgrown foliage, fleeing like a skittering ferret to break away. He casts limpid currents and shapeshifting shadows in his wake. Suddenly, the obscurities loom alive and Lucy shivers to think someone is coming to steal them away.

Lucy trembles. Once alone, questionable temerity turns terrible as a sudden crack from the plantation's old walnut tree weakens with age. As if in timely treason the seasoned bark balks and breaks with imploring cries against removing change. This is the most alone she has felt in all her life, a single second of a previous day.

Fortunately the notion of being alone has never been a matter to contemplate on Higg's farm. It frightens more than black widow spiders in the barn or water moccasin snakes swimming by her leg in the dark, but there is no turning back… too late. After the branch crashes and dies on the withdrawn terrain, she breathes in a hollow gasp and for a second her heart hesitates.

Fear's adrenaline pumps hard, absolute and unadulterated. Like a clamp on her gut against the grain or the drawing ache of a virulent strain it plunges her into a tragedy's play. Has an animal in the woods come to sup from the stream or come to prey? What if a wild wolf pack killed Cal and Mona, leaving them slain? Is this perilous and truly frightful risk to her family a big mistake? Reality strikes an ominous, dissonant chord to challenge the fray.

Cal, the steam engine conductor, leads the way. Lord loves a locomotive behemoth, so protective she's always felt safe. Mona transforms spirit, the beautiful bits of shiny, black coal, which fire the engine on Lucy's overloaded freight. With her loved ones out of sight, maybe never to be seen again, Lucy feels plain as produce goods, a naked avoirdupois pulling the weight of a burdensome chain. She looks right, left and back whence they came and went on their way. She considers moving her stationary feet, but they are glued in place.

Wringing her hands, she postpones her journey's initiation, scared immovable and she shrinks back from the din of primeval space. Evening chatter overwhelms, dithering in a perpetual bane. Locusts of late wane, but whizz more now wildly chiding a causal wave. Out of nowhere a cacophony of cantankerous crickets chant, no less inane. The intense din begins to come at her face and through her ears with a frenetic backbeat from rambunctious bullfrogs trumpeting as a trio on the bank. They sit on rocks belching brook side registering a bothersome bay. Even the haunting hoot of a cryptic whippoorwill is no longer the friendly companion he was during the day.

"Lawd give me strength an' keep us safe from hahrm." A quivering voice rattles through her head as emotions jump to a-jangle, when she starts to pray.

A past Sabbath message re-ministers from the pulpit bay. Remember Lot's wife relegated to a salty, pillared state? She stood condemned to stay that way for the rest of her days. No need to explain now what the preacher was trying to convey. Lucy did not dare qualify the predicament by looking back and risk her family's fate. She does not despair, but trusts in Providence and her own ingenuity to escape.

She's never seen the Hatchie River fork; there's never been a reason to head that way from the estate. If she is to find Cal and Mona, she must rustle up the gumption though, reasonably viable to anticipate. Brooding, Lucy plunges into her pocket at a pungent piece of onion crackling the golden, papery casing. Palms scrub the white, hard flesh underneath to increase the odor encapsulated. Rubbing the onion on her feet continues in syncopation with a panicky, perseverating sway. Dry saliva gulps hard down her throat from a cup of determination lifted up to partake. Finally, with gobs of grass and dirt gripped in fistfuls and thrown away, she musters the courage to break away.

"I set muhsef t'muh obje'tif an' back t'sane. No mattuh what, I gonna wear dis pawr life out t'save any chile o'mine from bein' sol' a slave!"

Divinely, a delicious peace in the evening's breeze begins to caress her ears with calming sounds like the babbling brook and windswept leaves rustling at play. She digs deep for resourceful buried for just such a day, bunches up her cotton garb, pulls the gingham skirt between her thighs, and twists it into a fat knot before tucking it at the waist. Precursor to winding westward due, Lucy is to lattice Grays Creek west gusseting, zigzag to tie up loose ends like corseted lace. Theoretically, this strategy is to put the enemy and dogs alike on a wild goose-chase, no need to erase their trace.

Palpitating scents of onion bits and pepper pinches upon her heels mitigates. Rigorous foot massaging claims cadence, intrepid the pace. Atop her head the trusty tub is held like a sturdy hat in place. Lucy curtsies with a cautious toe out as if getting ready to waltz with a prince at the king's ball, but not today. She peeks over and down below her foot, the murky water does not oblige navigation.

Down onto the dampness of the clay, down into a cold, silt creek bed she maneuvers clumsy, unsure and unsafe. She slogs along feeling out of her element and about to tumble down in a three-legged sack race. The coolness of the water feels invigorating at first; but the chill soon bites to the bone and becomes obnoxious, needling like hundreds of prickly pins poking in one combined ache. She winces and bites her tongue as a closed-mouth grimace defines the pain. Quarrelsome to a squatter, missteps go astray across slippery stones on the bottom and give her cause to harness stumbles with but a few decent scrapes.

Lucy skids across the slimy stream, tension mounting like a tightrope walker's death defying phrase. Smooth nuggets and jabs from paunchy pebbles trouble a slight splash she does not want displayed. Thankfully a tadpole plunks in with tiny legs to ease the noisy advantage. Cold as fingers in February on a crying cow's udders, the temperatures numb her knees to toes within the hour, but she stays the course, managing the mossy creek the rest of the way unfazed. Her determined features draw dramatic shadows in the mettle of the moonlight's chalky haze. Lucy conquers courage through experience with baby steps of faith. Dimensions of calm maturity start to unfold like a rose and blossom on her still youthful visage.

Just as God gave His son to save the world with grace, so Lucy surrenders, the victory won. She places at the Lord's feet their destiny fashioned to manifest… on the run. Fatal consequences at hand reprimand her in realization, mentally wrung. Contraband! Slave! Fugitive! Labels warp a walloping judgment and threats may name family as miscreants or a more sordid sentencing crime yet unsung. I know, as she sits before me, deliverance comes. Presently, Lucy looks up at me, pale and fading brown eyes.

"T's in d'watuh fo' d'longes' mile, feelin' d'numbin' col' through t'muh toes, but I be doin' what Cal say t'do, when d'nex' foe knockin' on muh do'. D'rec'ly I heahs hahrd rushin' watuh comin' lo' an' I drag muhsef brefless, heavin' 'n' shiv'rin' t'de sho'. Crawch't neah a tangl't mess o'buhrch an' buhrl'd, cypress knee, root awll e'spose', I took t'sittin' on d'tub uptuhrn't b'low. Like a Nuhrvous Nellie kinda duckin', lookin' ovuh muh sho'duh 'n' squattin' low, I wrings out muh skuhrt so as not t'make any nawse, kinda fawrsi-buh 'n' slow. Summuh's fawres' fostuhrs free rec'nition, fawrtitude, an' whiny, raspin' katydids retaliatin' t'sing a late summuh show. I takes a deep bref an' rubs onions on muh feet once mo'… still no sign o'Cal o'Mo', so I fo'bear 'til d'Lawd repawrt in His still, smawll vawce."

"I look' t'de Heavens an' saw nuffin', but branches ablur like hun'erds o'spin'ly spiduh legs, uptuhrn't, stiff 'n' gnawrl'd like d'dead 'n' col'. Whar did muh Mo' 'n' Cal go? I ain't yet t'know, so I waits 'n' waits an' prays some mawre, awll d'while dat impingin' feahs encroach like a stawrm goin' t'blow. S'pose I spen' a bit o'time recitin' muh *savin'* discawrse, but I keeps thinkin' I gonna git cotched an' break a sweat, col'. D'Lawd gonna provide d'refuge; deep down I knows."

Luckily, Lucy graduated from the school of hard-knocks and survival a decade ago in life. Rankling at adventure's approach like she yanked her Mama's apron as a child, still holding her positive cache cup and patience, albeit not watertight, was essential for this night. Where God sends His children, sovereign planting frames a plan He shan't deny. She stares west into the woods where secrets belie. Just then a bulky figure breaks branches to her right. If it isn't Cal and Mona, it is a big black bear lolloping into sight.

Fingers clasp tightly together in prayer as if to the reins of a runaway horse. "Lawd be praised fo' keepin' us on cawrse."

Lucy cautiously stood, puts the old tub, housing a couple of clothes and some bread on her head, no hesitation or remark. He motions in silence toward the Hatchie confluence north of Grays Creek cleft fork. She grabs Cal's muscular hand as he stands erect in a strapping stance and together the three step off the shore.

"Confawrm t'muh step, mahrk'd an' sho like we's one hawrse. Der yuh go. No need t'feah. We be fully on cawrse." Cal's encouragement reads easy as a Sunday morn. Environs indicative of a smooth current draw forth.

Mettle of the mighty without saying, "Forward." goes. The sinuous river rushes up headlong without proper introduction shown. Water floods around her like a riotous crowd of people rudely pushing onto a concourse. Cal and Lucy remain fused as galvanized steel on a sturdy scaffold, step by step as a family closer to freedom, so her confident demeanor and valor, once full of fear, by the same degrees rose. It is about one mile across, but largely dredged by steamboats, draught shallow. Her wet clothes cling, in tired folds, exemplifying elderly skin sagging chest to toes.

Cal is the protective ox plowing rows. Lucy the planter, deeply seeding with love of Mona bagged in tow. They trudge for hours past fields, farms and knolls, while Cal still carries Mona and Lucy her tub with their tiny treasure trove. He points across the rising bluff towards a mulberry grove.

"Lawd knows we's a so' eyed sight, I's headin' in fuhrs' t'see if'n dis heah's a trigguh happy guy. When I be cleahr, come through wif Mo' in due time. Say to 'em dis, 'Fo' safe passage yuhr gonna cook 'n' clean an' d'like.' Now doncha feel a fright."

Cal kisses their cheeks and strolls brazenly to the field bathed in an ephemeral, bluish backlight. Multiple campfires that dot the grounds earlier for dinner are doused, when soldiers retire for the night. Their smokiness spreads thin and wide. A filmy smolder in the air blocks twinkling stars adding eerie fingers between the pines and across the luminous sky. He lifts his arms straight out to his sides, palms up presenting nothing to hide.

She squints as the darkness sucks him in, then she hears a steadfast command that makes her quickly clutch Mona a little more tightly, "Halt. Who goes there, so late this night?"

Cal stammers at the sound and squints for sight. "I-I'se unahrm't 'n' full ready t'enlis' wif d'Union 'n' pledge t'fight."

The soldier counters commands, promulgating from behind a hedge post on high. "Come ahead slow with no sudden moves, 'cause I got you dead in my sights." She watches from behind the weeds with the taste of tension and trepidation at the corner of her mouth, chalky-white from spittle well-dried. Cal walks forward to the soldier behind a ridgeline.

Grabbing low hanging boughs to hide by reaching up from beneath, she steadies herself to have a closer eye. Her right palm cups Mona's head for the ride, whilst folds of fabric hold her closer and weigh down her side. From the journey's onset intensified fears have given birth and now hang as heavy as her child, thus preoccupying her mind. She feels ravenous and thirsty at the same time as her stomach gurgles and her throat goes tight. She takes the tub in tow on her left, wide. Her voice is dry and full of prickly thorns like treading onto an Arizona desert covered with snakes and cacti.

Lucy takes a yawning breath through her nose and holds it, a sucked in sigh of courage and valor, ready to die for her child. Stepping out in faith tonight feels like plummeting over a craggy cliff for a precious pearl dive. She taps her toe onto the clearing as if testing a façade frozen with February ice. Though summer sweat drips in ribbons down hersides, her foot hovers in the air belied. It floats like frosty clouds suspended over a glacial crevasse, yet set to crack wide as the woods, if she dares-the-space to occupy. Both mother and babe would drown in an ocean of purpose, hither to be identified. She trembles nonstop in place like a wilting leaf in a tempest about to fly from its stem, give up and die. Furthermore, she wants to bolt, find a burrow, and hide like a long-eared, black-tailed jackrabbit hearing the howl of a pack of wolves... terrified.

The rest of her body follows later, tempering like tender blowing easy onto a brush of kindling in hopes it ignites. Susceptibility swirls as smoke from a fire beginning to blaze inside. Irrepressible freedom's desire pushes itself to the forefront of her mind. Danger does not deter nor does a dire hardship deny. The howling slave hound's garrulous alarm would not have advanced a stronger desire for freedom to her stride.

Suddenly, she is fleeing the fuse that ignites dynamite's wire. Faster and faster she runs, heaving shallower, but almost out of breath in the brisk cantering charge of a combatant into line of fire. Her heart wants to fly from her chest, sever the Union line without her and Mona, and fling itself at last on an altar of freedom's pyre. Recognizing the crest of salvation, she slows her sprint to finally pad fatigued as a footsore pup mid-meadow, the heat to her head more hurriedly on the rise. Deeper anxiety attacks, when the picket barks his order with intensity, ebon effaces her eyes. Lucy lifts them in a blind prayer destined to the skies.

The faceless voice belts powerful from the picket's post, "Who goes there this fine night?"

Words of a sensible nature might manage on an ordinary occasion's inquisition just fine. However, breathless, bumbling mumbles put a placket in pronouncement as vertigo shoved a shunt into her practiced preamble like an unholy amount of acrid vinegar inside the throat climbs and hammers like a sledge on railroad ties.

"Beggin' … safe passage t'wuhrk uh… ti…" Her voice trails off and she stares into the blackness flummoxed, blank as a bungling mime.

A nasty case of collusive fear and nerves' misery monitors the tolling stop. A change in circumstance in the breadth of time it takes to snap one's fingers rushes to her head harsh and hot. As devaluing darkness veils all distinction she blinks in opposition to the endless inkiness. She is no longer able to see her hand before her and the tunneling vision spirals smaller and smaller likening to a blackened dot. Lucy's knees betray her weight; though, oddly enough, she was barely thought to fill a large stewpot. There she collapses out-splayed, suffering to fall like a spoonful of mashed succotash, buttered with a pat of child on top. Thankful Grace attends to spawn relief beneath her with hollow stalks. The yellowed scape, feathery dry from a summer drought now at an end, cover the ground knee-high in pale tawny fawns. They rustle when her steps cross the open plain, but carefully crinkle now, bending to break her fall like a softening mound of newly cut straw.

The saving fingers of salvation stretch, entwining destiny's design to arrive at a perfect juncture defined in His time. Lil Mona's sling slowly sags, so our Lord's ubiquitous hand can ease the hard fall's crime. Verging on anachronistic sensations, not catatonic, Lucy feels out of time, possibly caught, but categorically she is oxygen deprived blind. The wooden tub bonks a hollow thump by her body before it rolls on by; less of life than she, the contents trailing out, while blood drains from her face before it too clunks down of exhaustion to expire.

The guard yells out. "Sir looks like we got another one wontin' to cross the line."

"F" Company was covering the picket duty. Detailed this night of the division were brothers, John and Davy Marzee, Charlie Green and Isaac Free. When reminiscing with the men on one of their many marches, Lucy retells her ordeal with grins and giggles of glee.

"The God o'Heaven sho' do have quite d'sense o'humor. Now, don't He?" She had just found out the man on duty, when she crossed the threshold, answered to "Free". Discovering, she hunted them out and she and Mona prettily thanked each one of them immediately.

Arbitrary to announcement, the Union pickets clothe their important responsibility with absolute power untapped. Their fingers grip the shining stock of their readied muskets, which must always remain loaded and capped. They walk their rounds alone or in twos, until sounds and shadows connect to expose or perhaps to trap.

Warning takes prospect on plans of attack, where adversaries lurk you must stop or catch. With no meekness of character the terribly gallant groups of three to four soldiers move, paces marked three to four rods apart, thither they encircle their elongated laps. Long, weary marches cannot beg to pardon the sentinel, who will not yet see sleep before he takes up arms as the company watchman.

General Sanderson, Colonel Davis, and other officers let her stay as a nurse, laundress and cook in agreement complete. Soon Lucy is transforming common rations into well-rounded meals with herbs from the wild, which make for mightly tasty delicacies. She would whip up some fried ham or mush smothered with molasses, plus ash-baked sweet potatoes and dandylion greens. Not stopping short on a simple main course, the officers received dried peaches or hot buttered corn pones, incomplete without some freshly parched, hot black coffee with sweetener and a little cream. Except when in battle or bivouac, officers' stores comprise a wider range, often afforded with their monetary means.

PURPOSE
BEYOND REPOSE

Cal is given orders with a crew of four. They lay logs perpendicular with sand to corduroy roads in lower, swampy spots and reconstruct rails ripped by Rebel hoards. These tasks are crucial to maintaining the military's supply source. Lucy's lids blink in dawn's half-light and the hubbub of the corp. She's been out cold, since last report, camouflaged with Mona at her side truncating a few smooth, sycamores. Health bred by rest, water and calm reform, God's grace has endured them to morn. Lucy begs the pardon of a passing soldier to attempt her rehearsed speech once more. In all honesty she has intention of securing work with a Union regiment, her original assurance repeated quickly before the plea is cut short.

I venture the assertion that Dr. Magnus Brucker was promoted on account to heal, but a tad bugged and bewildered. At first implication toward her he immediately spends his spuriously abrupt demeanor. Heard tell in the rumor mill, the regiment's original surgeon resigned; rent on demoralizing horrors, happens to the best in times of war. Brucker toughened up as doctor to the entire corp, honoring solo, a month plus to his dedication and valor. Thankfully, two more surgeons arrived in due course, accompanied by General Hurlburt, men needed sorely. Brucker, McPheeters and Byrn, respectfully work as surgeons for Tennessee regiments in the brigade stationed near Bolivar city's core. Outspoken in suggestion, Chaplain John Rogers champions Lucy to come on board as bivouac cook and field nurse, Aid-De-Camp of the corp. Other officers, Will and John Davis in specific, brothers in Company "F", quickly trumpet horns for her assitance with full support.

The valiant volunteers of the 23rd Union defenders are variously comprised of comrades connected by their steamboat livelihood pursuits and in respect of one another they fight as hard as they work. All those folks hail from Indiana border counties, Floyd Clark, Harrison and Crawford. As well as other actual brothers within the troops, they correspond as kin shoulder to shoulder. Excellent are their dispositions with patriotism, loyalty and integrity of the highest honor. In their prompt response to Lincoln's critical call, they chose to leave no room for personally prejudiced rights, who would be keeping ambition's score or harboring thoughts of possible business gains or losses south to north.

Preservation and perpetuation of the Union and the Constitution, for which it stands, predominately prevail within their hearts and minds. They selected officers from their own number to command, almost without exception straight from their original line. Providence enlisted this company of men to instill inspiration and confidence from their commanders as friends and colleagues for life. Discipline and efficiency maintain to effect of the regiment from major general and on down the line.

"I membuhs d'kindly eyes o'Chaplin Roguhs, blue as a calm sea, no wind ablowin'. Yuh know, I nevuh see him sew a stitch o'sin; awlways preachin' on d'Sabbef, b'fo' an' afta battuhs, an' t'any othuh God feahin' sich'ation derein. When etuhrn'ty unfol's, he gonna have many a stahr in his crown o'rejoicin'. I gits a gran' repawrt on de mannuh o'charactuh fo' awll dem off'suhrs an' men in d'23ʳᵈ, whethuh I be comin' o'goin'. D'wahrmes' symp'thy fo' awll suffuhin' be d'mahrk o'der true Christian Spir't."

"Pastuh Roguhs 'n' Colonel Sanduhrson be d'ones, though dat hep't d'doctuhs 'n' offisuhs un'erstan' I be fit fo' d'field o'nuhrsin'. I wuhrks fo' d'doctuhs 'n' offisuhs from dat day t'de en' o'dat "Great Unpleasantess" on d'wahr o'sin. Dey done give us clothes, food, an' shoes an' protects us from churlish evuhdouhs, but I nevuh see'd a soljuhs pay rationin', duhrin' d'thick o'it. Cawrse, dat no mattuh, when Mo' safe I knows d'good Lawd gonna provide in d'en'."

"Lawd knows, d'cup we drinks on dis heah Earf 'venchly gits good an' bad fill't. I knows a peck o'truhbuhs boun' t'commence on accoun' we's considuhed cont'r'ban' still. We's prob'ly in d'eye o'de stawrm, I 'spec's right about den, but I be ready t'face d'squall in a lion's den o'a huhr'cane wind, if'n it be God's will."

They sleep in a tiny tent, suiting their size near the back of many that dot the field with thick cotton canvas, white as cream. About ten of the tents near theirs house musicians that practice by the crackle of the evening fires before they go to sleep. They are friendly and famously affable, so Lucy and Mona too, became quite neighborly. After sermons Chaplain Rogers is always grateful for their accompaniment to make the hymns, for a lack of a church, resonate through the camp more heavenly.

"Dey's a few boys black as night on dem fidduhls, cuhluhr'ts from N'Awlbany by d'Ohio Rivuh runnin' long souf o'Indianny. Dey claims dey wuhrks freed an' pay a smawll squattuh's fee. When dis heah wahr be ovuh, I's gonna go der wif Mo', jus' t'see."

At General Sherman's behest the band is always ready for songs that motivate the men to a patriotic display. Songs like The Star Spangled Banner or The Battle Hymn of the Republic blasted as loudly as can be and any other time in between it is commanded to rally encouragement or signify specific duties, come what may. Back in July of 1862, when the enemy was within eave's-dropping earshot to a slingshot's throw, the enemy's band induces to play. General Sherman, stiff as starch atop his horse, incites an even brassier set of tunes from his musicians harness heroic inducements to a fervor for Yankees heading to the fray. This strategy most certainly bolstered his battling to blast the Rebel grays.

"When dey's 'laxin' in recr'ation dem music boys plays often, sad 'n' low, when dey's homesick an' fas' 'n' boist'rous, when dey's a vic'try." Lucy waved her hands up and out in a band leader's swinging measure, slowly, then quickly, cocked her head down to the right and spoke out of the side of her mouth with a softer, sweetened memory.

"Sometime', when dem music boys stahrts t'talk 'bout dem Rebuhs, it be a bit shockin' t'impruhpri'ties, but still rathuh fun 'n' juicy. Why ev'n when dey wharn't playin' fo' d'mil't'ry, dey was heppin' revive droopin spir'ts wif bubbly beats."

"I gits t'knowin' d'music boys 'vench'ly, 'cause dey hep d'amb'lance git d'injuhred defenduhrs, dyin' 'n' dead outta hahrms way an' off d'fiel'. Yuh know Doc' M'Pheetuhs brothuh, Willy, fifuh fo' d'ban', rally his boys t'give us a han'… o'two o'three. Hep't us wif d'woun'ed, when we's sawrly in need."

"Cawrse, ovuh time I gits t'know purt neah awll dem folks by name. Why, yuh couldn't shake a stick for yuh's t'smack some boy by d'name o'Willy. Shuck it awll, three stew'rds at d'hospituh hit dat stake. Two dozen mawr in Comp'ny "F"… give o'take. I ain't 'bout t'zaj'rate! Still sees 'em up t'Indy, when d'Gran' Ahrmy o'de Republic has a meetin' date.

Dey use'ly come wif der brothuhs an' we haf a go at d'regalin' vict'ry tales. Lemme see heah, what boys muh mem'ry wajuh t'claim? Der's Gawrge 'n' Willy Kintuh, Frank 'n' Willy Creamuh, Phil 'n' Will Devaney, Will 'n' Isaac Pahrchese, Sol 'n' Will Bliss an' de fines' Union Cap'ns, Willy 'n' John Davis. Yuh's boun' t'see half a dozen Johns 'n' Gawrges dat awll glance d'rection'ly, when yuh cawll out der name." Lucy sharply looks left, then right, then toward me and we both grin with a quiet chuckle at the game.

SURVIVAL HONED

Much like life on the acreage privileged by Grays Creek, mornings begin quiet and serene under Milky Way's calm covering, when babes sleep awash in dreams. Rousing report's stamp wakefulness on dawn, contrasted extraordinary, when unzipping each morn in the military. Rapid movement resounds to the bugler's reveille beat. Still deeply aslumber, snug on a rubber bed with a bit of cotton blanket feeling fully free, Mona softly purrs as a contented kitty. Mama tenderly tweaks her toddling treasure in merriment's glee and pecks her with a spirited buss on the cheek. Together, mother and daughter oblige the day in elation as new found hope and love pervade air with vibrant colors and smells a might sweeter.

Her trusty tub never far, Aunt Lucy never dilly-dallies to duty. The wooden bucket's hemp bracelet rubs as it hangs slightly scratching. Lucy forages hickory nuts from the hardened branches of trees near the gully, plucks huckleberries, plump and fresh, off bushes by a back road and rummages dandelions other robust herbs found growing wild in the area resourceful for cooking and healing as occasions may need. She gathers hunks in handfuls with speed, mindful of being; she has a young child to feed.

She pokes her head out; crickets are humming slower, which pleases on a breeze in the late summer heat. Two dashing blue jays jerk her eye to the wood as they flit flirtatiously from a mighty oak, not yet mature, to a taller, neighboring, toughened up hickory. Lucy peers left and then right before stepping outside with one eye still closed in sleepy agreement. On all sides white men wiggle out of white cotton broadcloth astir, ready to greet the day, just as she. Somewhere down in Mississippi, boll weevils are writhing in white cotton balls left unattended in the Deep South seat.

The felicitous fife and drum will soon call breakfast, but Mona and Lucy sing and skip to their own beat, hand in smaller hand, a blissful stride of tightly sewn seams. Beaming and chiming up a cheerful greeting, they bob and nod, counting each tented row laid straight and neat.

"One two, buckle muh shoe. Three fo', shut d'dawr. Fi' sic, pick up d'stick." She shared a few verses of rhyme 'n' wit taught to Missus Chairs' child during playtime sittings. The little one joyfully grabs a discarded piece of kindling, shows it to her mama with a grin.

"That's right, muh lil punkin." Lucy giggles. They skip off dragging sticks, kicking up dirt, and laughing in stitches.

The encampment is aflutter with men doing various duties, utterly busy as bees, and Lucy, no exception, heaves water from the river to the northeast. Within the hour she prepares a timely repast of fried ham, fresh berries and cornpones for the officers' breakfast, and of course, a sizable pot of piping hot, black coffee. The duo happily heads to the hospitals to roll bandages and wash wounds clean. Sonorous notes parade a piece from the band in the background, as is the norm, usually.

Pages of an appropriate, eventful, and effervescent ensemble escalate for guard mounts during the inspecting dress cavalcade. Brave sentinels get dismissed and quickly replaced. Drills to dinner, meetings to preaching, roll calls in the morning and evening, and of course, the great dress review, all commence and dismiss with a fife, drum, and/or bugle display.

Watching the spectacle of rank and file is something to comprehend. Frock coats, white gloves and sashed uniforms eminently adorn soldiers marching abreast in grand revolution, illustrious to impress. Musicians send out their measured, dress-marching best. The early sun gleams gilden off shiny bayonets. Pride of position and Union patriotism buff up the buttons polished on every chest. Each company follows in succession, when the reports for roll-call present. The gallant Colonel William Sanderson salutes and draws his noble sword from its scabbard to put the soldiers through practice and tests.

Lucy and Mona mosey downtown to the hospitals established at the houses of worship by General Hurlburt's hardy men of the 10th, their heads satiated with music. Methodist, Episcopal and both small Presbyterian churches give ward to wounded and ailing from the bloody battles of Shiloh and Corinth. Merry Mona shadows her mama from sun-up satisfied, until twilight's a trickle and still she shines like a copper penny newly mint. Together they possess an inexhaustible source of positive dispositions, which illumine every task and soul with good-humor's rippling trills and gracious, spiritual hymns.

Lucy does everything under the sun with her daughter by her side, snug as a two bugs in a rug. They plunge blue woolen uniforms to launder in a soapy scrub, sew glittering, gilt buttons to shirts with a polishing rub, and cook tasty, downhome mid-west grub to full appeasement of the officers' hub. She is happy to cater indulgent favors, since they took her family in, when they were stuck. Regular regiments in the east may have a Cook Major that makes a comely, monthly sum, but the majority of men from the 23rd volunteers are left for eats to their own, unskilled bumluck. Women are not as prevalent among field camps, but their feminine touch compliments through maternal mildness mixed with pluck.

Her old family recipes saturate the air in wafting sniffs. Fresh food is delivered by rail in quite regular succession. Bread, bacon, dried beans, potatoes, sugar, coffee, rice, molasses, least not mentioned, vegetables and dried fruits aplenty, divvied out after Lucy and Mona prepare and fix. Liberal leftovers make hot soup's special healing, which they spoon in to waiting weak lips. Medicine is meted out to ameliorate disabled and sick soldiers throughout their hospital shifts. Four hospital stewards, three surgeons, two nurses (Lucy and Mona) and the singular chaplain, sounds copious enough to make rounds to all the patients, but to hundreds of men that kept coming in continual streams, there are wounds to clean, bandages to change and medicines to dispense every minute.

Patients, doctors, stewards and officers as well, are sorely glad they are there to assist. For all of these men that have been in harm's way, charity of Providence does indeed exist. Quite the fledgling nurse, little merry Mona ministers and sings songs down each row, a pat-pat with her left hand on top and a gentle squeeze with her right on the bottom of a sickly soldier's palms, mimicking Mama Lucy at each rubber blanket or cot.

"Hope t'day gonna find yuh feelin' bettuh." Mona merrily twitters as she sidles up to a soldier's cot. "I gots a song t'sing fo' yuh, if yuh wants..." She sang a small, made up ditty, "D'rain gonna fawll an' raise o'purty squawll."

At other bedsides a forehead receives a moistened cloth sopped in cool water or a thatched reed fan waved, when it gets too hot. As common consolation they sing sweet strains, mother/daughter duets of lyrical lullabies or soulful, rustic river songs. They serenade others for hours somberly soft, as the Grim Reaper calls upon last breaths from martyred men's mouths. It is strange all this agony and death does not affect them in disgust like some in witness to a roadside sot. Quite the contrary, they become accustomed with all the convalescents and grace their presence with pleasant dispositions in grateful gobs.

"Sometimes d'Pastuh be prayin' wif us, offuhrin' up d'ahrd'nt prayuhs fo' d'mos' tragic scene o'de lamentabuh lot." Lucy no longer cherishes her window's repose of the past, but prays fervently for each man to God. Each day Lucy and Mona clasp hands. There is no regret the chosen swap.

"Heal dese men an' hahrm come t'em not. Watch ovuh us in d'name o'de Lawd."

Golden glints spark inside the iris of her eyes and glimmer, when she speaks of the chaplain, always willing to lend a helping hand. Tender attention to services and regular prayer meetings is announced weekly in camp. He takes time as need demands to counsel folks individually, whither hours marching hither and yon across this land. The chaplain also augments guided hymns by the band. Lucy serves side by side with him in the various church hospitals and while on bivouac; during bloody fighting in the field, inches from terrible, swift shot trying every triage trial hand to hand. God animates those sacrificing in service on a field of fire with His presence as only He can.

Speechless seconds off into space, Lucy contemplates. "Yuh know, I wayjuhs awll dem battuhs be lost on Mem'ry Way to cawll awll o'dem up at any given place. Wahrs be drea'fuhl fo' bofe sides an' ev'ry race, but I 'membuhs d'speshuh folks an' d'thin's we do on differ'nt days like d'fuhrst battuh o'when we's relyin' solely on God's Grace."

Her eyes tear a bit as if she thinks of the calming, courageous countenance of Chaplain Roger's face. I stare at her intently not knowing just what to say, so I take a bite of an apple slice, a composing sip of tea… first rate. I am dearly grateful for her memories, so until she is ready, I wait.

Eventually she clears her throat of emotion and starts up again.

"A rare man indeed fo' d'ahrs he labuhr'd an' d'love o'de Lawd he awlwus freely gave. D'kindes' an' mos' fo'bearin' man o'de cross fo' men t'be call't brave. He huhrald fo'de Pottuh's Field now, gone t'his grave, an' I specs he finally be gittin' his full hepin' o'Glawry's fame."

Lucy's lips compress in nodding agreement of the same. I can still heahr Pastuh preachin' wif a rich, thunduh bol' soun', 'Be fai'fuh soljuhs o'Jesus an' o'dis country. See us through t'vic'try an' d'safety o'God's will be done as we take up a cross o'take up a crown. Amen in Jesus name.' I look t'his esampuh through d'wahr on how t'b'have. So wuhrthy 'n' zealous 'n' full, his cup ovuhflow in faith. I sho' look fawrwuhrd t'shakin' his hand an' a wahrm embrace on Judgmen' Day."

The noble chaplain follows his regiment assisting every battle array. He raises stretchers of wounded men in his arms and carries them away from devilish arenas, bespattered and dripping blood down his shirt and trousers, shells whizzing past at every pace. Hours upon days he cares for and prays for the suffering soldiers, as well as admonishing the achievements of his faithful, patriotic flock, ever imminently brave. Particulars of eloquence were credited in reporting glory by staunch General Sherman after Shiloh and Corinth's embattled display. Knit together like even stitches, family in company, regiment, and bastioned brigade, which included Lucy and her daughter, praying each day. Their deepest faith is not yet put to the test by fiercest cannonade.

PUBLIC PRUNING

What a North Easter knows about the Western Theatre warrants review. The subject tweaked onto the scene from newsprint weeklies like corn kernels sitting on a sizzling, hot skillet pop out every which way you lean. Multiple rumor mills crop up from sutlers and traveling medicine shows, notwithstanding a few ladies chatterboxing in quilting bees. Every town and tongue takes considerable timbre of speech associated in some form with the war's commerce, from the paid labor of industry versus an agrarian economy at the expense of slaves in theme. Opinionated souls can't help but be embroiled in the machinations of hostilities, whether for the greater good or self-serving recriminations of the cause turned ugly. The big city presses and *Harpers Weekly* as well, dole out pieces of the pie in divisive black and white commentary to update the bulletin hungry. One could easily follow generals' strategies from point 'A' to point 'B'.

A pantheon of WestPoint Generals commandeer as the heated conflagration sweeps. Battalion base camps headquarter within the Border States, which comprises parts of Tennessee. Lincoln applauded men who volunteered to fill the need. His pleas came on the heels of firm and united action reaching west in the fullness of time by horse, buggy, railway wheels and waterway's speed. An extreme priority for soldiers was expressed by Bolivar, Tennessee and Louisville, Kentucky. Enough to keep rivers and rails defended and clear for any transports was the objective imperative.

General Grant in his consummate collected manner and stockier build, chest to hip, though slightly stooped, shoulders burdened and bent. He pours over his maps, whilst converting into a clear, connoisseur of cigars, always in his tent with one lit. By curious and unpredictable acts of Providence he becomes butted up to reticent topbug lickety-split, an enigma of unconventional fashion towit. His right-hand man and unyielding shield was an unstinted militaristic general, Sherman, with his lantern jaw, quite truculent, he sits. Ever straight-horsed ready and chaffing at the bit, he befits the role of sole confidante for Grant during war's rifled pits. Conspicuous others of note too, honoring the ledger along the way are promising McPherson, tall of stature, Wallace, thin in the lip, Logan, coal-black eyes, mustached thick, dimpled at the chin, plus a half dozen diverse others coming and going to advance at the whip.

After losses at Shiloh and Corinth, restoration to divisional strength and protecting secured supplies in the existing and newly launched headquarters, and maintaining highly important supply lines domineers. Runaway slaves are employed to accomplish this feat. Once the tide of the war broadened and original policies on interference with property and contraband counter an about face by Federal decree, Grant recruits many for manual labor, hired on to succor his dwindling military. Hundreds of exslaves repair the Mississippi Central, not soldiers, but at a worker's fee.

How to handle slaves in Union camps deems quite contradictory in lettered sentiments shared and war's reports from the field. The opinions of men in charge, pole to pole change diametrically with the ebb and flow of political tide as each battle's victory may intensify or yield. Barely six months ago, accepting slaves through lines with a pass to be free, utilizing them for work or enlistment, and/ or keeping them at camps to be reclaimed was deemed plain, contraband, reasonably believed. During the first half of '62, slaves escape by hundreds for freedom's dream. An exodus exploded by '63, when struggling thousands fled in need. A manic flurry of correspondence with as many variances in disposition flew between Generals, officers and Lincoln's team for the purpose of ameliorating political, social and inevitable, economic frustration and misery. The government does not want to make this war about slavery, the South insists it is about this issue alone, *property*, and thus dig in their heels.

Personal moral and social codes control and inflame each to their own standard of government, snarling with rants about tradition and mimicking religious and political tenets, kept more strictly than believed. The Midwest too, reaps racist within groups garnering black and white newsprint, insensitive, slanderous, and defrauding. Reporters and lawyers built up the city's distaste on incident to an imprisonable, skirmishing riot in New Albany. More than 200 already freed, black citizens are run out of town. Back in Indiananapolis, Governor Morton assists abolitionists with enthusiastic, valiant testimony. Initially he receives praise, but chastisement from Gary on down to New Albany succeeds and he fails in his final vestige.

When persecution rears an ugly head to benefit from opportunity, some choose spiritual, guidance; other souls take advantage of weaker women, children and slaves at camps in the countryside and prisons from west to the east. On the eastern shores, mothers beg palpable in the Carolinas, uprising in the streets for bread to feed war's children hungry and needing. The chaotic combination becomes combustible, a hand-crafted powder keg of calculating criticism indeed. Unchecked Northern farmers fleeced by greatly reducing labor prices, when hiring escapees. Aggressive competition increased, while multiples of more passive people turned the other cheek.

Politics is sad and vehement work, when committees refuse to agree. Specifically notable, some legislators lobby in loathing, vociferously to denounce emancipation's decree. They waggle pointing fingers at Civil War's participation trophies, not a few turncoats drum up additional warring beats. Hysteria of insane proportions towards arming unchained slaves as enlisted men is proposed by some in Congress as a highly, unpleasant possibility. Their arguments can not deny in the end that extra arms, although rather reluctantly, assist the means. The demand to increase and complete state's troop quotas carries on as the war rages into '63, because America cannot stop bleed.

ROSES STILL BLOOM

"Cal be buil'in' dem roads, bridges, fawrti'cations, gun-pits an' d'like b'fo' he gonna head ovuh t'suhrve fo' d'cuhluh'd troops o'Tenn'see fo' awhile. He be wuhrkin' wif a Hallelu' smile. Listen heah, though not t'gethuh, we bofe done been down pas' d'Miss'sip' line. He sho' nuff thought God an' d'Union gonna save our humbuh b'hinds. Cawrse, we rightly 'specs anyhow, God be on der side."

Cal's muscular physique makes him mighty favored as one of those able bodied, jack of all trades fellows sorely needed. The first six months sees him sweating hard service, reconstructing railroads and digging ditches in danger's way for the Union military. He digs in the dirt daily, proud as a papa to be part of the fight to be free. I don't know how he seems to have quite a serious face, when attending to focus, yet quick to draw a laugh alternatively. When President Lincoln is so bold to enact the Emancipation Proclamation, Cal finally got to wear the blues I believe, while fighting for the U. S. Colored Infantry.

Patriotic all is given in proper support through blood, sweat and guts for the Defender's side. The manly father and provider that he is Cal spares tidbits of rations and relinquishes most of his money to Lucy and Mona, mollifying incidental needs for the first two months of the fight. Fulfilling his purpose vigorously, he lodges with groups of laboring men on site, be it river, railway, or rigging tied. He barters for evenings to reconnect with his family just beyond the fairgrounds past the grove, when his schedule can comply.

One evening Cal retraced their escape path to the abandoned plantation of Albert and Prudence Chairs with some men on the sly. Just as any quick withdrawal leaves valuables behind, there scavenge plenty of garden goods, cords of wood, work tools, stores of canned food and other materials to help them get by. A time or two willing, he brings back an apron, sewing notions, and spices. Weeks later he shucked an extra linsey, woolsey shirt and a casual cornhusk doll, from shelf out of sight. The mini, matching bonnet and gingham frock were still intact for his daughter's delight.

They both know Albert Chairs will petition for his property fit to be tied. Daily prayers and, when time allows rendezvous outside the campsite. Cuddling reenergizes in wee hours secluded on the grass under pristine twinkles of star-filled light. As evening shade settles in special, Lucy and Cal witness spiritual gifts, radiant, Perseid meteor showers, and a multi-colored cloud-trail surprise. Assuming God is sharing their victory with late Fourth of July fireworks; they lay mesmerizing with soft, oohing and ahhing cries and thank God for the blessing of the "falling skies" before they kiss goodnight... They didn't know it would signify their last good bye.

"Lawd we know'd you set us on d'path dat's right. Keep guidin' us fo' yo' puhrpose in Prov'dence' light.

Amen in Jesus Precious Sight. Give hugs t'lil Mo' fo' me." Cal spoke with love and kissed Lucy goodbye. A welling wash overcame her eye and dropped in a splashy tear on her aproned thigh.

—⁄ \⦆—

The autonomy of Lucy's New Albany kitchen is acreage apart from where she began and admires a wholly different view for repose. The curtain is tea stained to an off-white eggshell dressing the window where the eye follows. We walk out the back door and down a couple of crumbly, concrete steps, stopping just before the flourishing display she has toiled to grow. A tall, slatted white trellis built by veterans from Sanderson's Post arches overhead with dozens of cerise-red roses. I comment on their beauty and fragrance, but in regrettable penalty, I ask if this is something Cal has made, due to the muscular comments Lucy had made, this is the case one might suppose. A narrow gravel walkway clean through the center about fifteen feet long led to a small shanty shed sitting in the back leaning, a bit sad all alone.

"No, dat be fashioned by John Nic'uhs an' d'felluhs from d'Post. D'rec'ly he be comin' home. Dat las' prayuh t'Heaven be d'las' time I sees Cal so close. He be pow'rful good man though, no tahrnish on dat mem'ry fo' sho'. Reckon a passel o'good men went t'de Lawd from shahrp-shootuhs ahidin' high 'n' low neah Bol'vahr from infuhr-nuh, skuhrmishin' rows. Only d'Good Lawd dat sees awll dat mess know... We'll meet agin on d'Judgement Day, I 'spose." I mumble my apologies and try to change the subject to a topic not full of woe. I quickly ask what happened to her previous owners, Missus Prudence and Master Albert Chairs, since they opted for the southern road.

Lucy meticulously prunes aging petals as she tours the trellis. Agreeable beauties are snipped and bunched in a breathtaking bloom of the senses, compliments owned only by roses so fresh. After rummaging in a cupboard she produces a crystal-clear, Mason jar, perfect in size for just cut stems. Water from the tap quenches them thoroughly and she assembles some greenery before decorating the windowsill where the bread pan had been.

"Der yuh go, purty flawuhrs, awlwus brings a swee'ness t'de hahrdes' soul." She stands back to survey with her arms atop her apron, angled akimbo. "D'truf of it is, I don' rightly know, but I tells yuh dis much fo' sho'. One day I be wuhrkin in d'hospituh, puttin' on a clean ban'age or sumpin' I 'spose. We'se in Bol'var yet, when de Chaplain saddles up 'side me slow, like he gots a secr't an' stahrts t'talkin' ser'ous 'n' low."

'D'offisuhs jus' has a meetin', he says. "Seems de Pos' Massa been busy sendin' awll sawrts o'lettuhs o'wahr t'day. I stops muh ban'age wrappin' mid fol', stills muh hands an' keeps muh head down an' jus' moves muh eyes his way. Some folks been askin' 'bout you an' Mona, a felluh by d'name o'Chairs tryin' t'stake his claim. Muh hahrt jump up cleahr t'muh throat an' cotched muh bref like I'se hit wif a pebbuh in a tin can, tahrgit game. I keep muh neck ben', lookin' at d'ban'age waitin' like muh han' done gone lame."

"See it been long 'bout two month' gone, an' I be hopin' he nevuh find us agin. Pastuh put a han' t'muh back an' whispuhs, 'D'Good Lawd is on ahr side. It gonna be okay.'

"It seems d'subjec' o'dislawl' procliv'ties don' sit well wif grace, so Gen'ral Grant gots plenny a page t'say. He don' look too kindly on folks thinkin' d'Union soljahs an' hep be sumpin dey could take. Cawrse, dat's what Chaplain Roguhs tol' me d'gist o'dat lettuh fo'ward due gonna say. I dinna know if I gonna cry, but I be feelin' so 'lated wif joy, I be clappin' muh hands an' jumpin' up an' down a bit in muh place, but secr'tly I be wontin' t'see d'look on Massa Chairs' face. Cawrse, awll I can do is shout 'Hallelu' in praise an' grab d'Chaplain full on d'face." Lucy looks at me, clasps her hands tightly, looks to the ceiling and thanks Jesus again with another grin of praise.

SKIRMISHING SOJOURNS

Two cycles of the moon had phased, since their escape. Lucy Higgs' motto thus far was to maintain an amiable disposition and it has remained intact during their time in the Union camp to date. Her demeanor always did hover happily near alacrity anyway. Anticipation of field nursing duty during skirmishes to come, however, hews hunks from good humor's silver lining on any given day. Favoring nerves against the unknown fate of men and the Union causes her normally congenial mood to dissipate. The generals know they are ready, stretching assurance to encompass the entire brigade to enter into a considerable, southern campaign. Lucy wants to run back to her window's repose on Higg's estate and pray, but it is too far away.

It's not that the Union isn't ready as combatants or men. She has every confidence in them, despite the stress. Lucy and Mona have seen them drill and practice, capable to impress. The soldiers' initial instability has been reharnessed full strength months back and redressed to the admirable condition of a solid regiment. The problem stems from her growing loyalty and attachment to them. Lucy surrendered all in a corset-tightened, time frame as happens with any set of brothers sent to serve and protect.

It happens with *any* folks that work and connect twentyfour-seven, facing dread and breaking bread. Life is more than adventure's eager adrenaline racing around her heart and head, pumping up a fine and furious fettle. Unimpeachable comradery and friendship shape and bend, simply by packing gear and food in wagons for upcoming marathon marches, bivouacs and battles ahead. She has to trust and accept where they are being led… by Providence or by death.

Before troops tag Jacksonville, Tennessee on foot, they first traverse by train. Some rails have seen grisly attacks from a few deserters and the rampaging animus of Confederate raids, but boatloads of people and freight moving by land quickly is best done this way. The gleaming engine sits steaming; smoke's rising up from its stack, inordinate the columns of tufted gray. Lucy lifts Mona into Thomas Lane's locomotive arms loading up an ample, boxcar's bay. John Highfill hoists her inside with the strong hauling hand and a smile on his face. Lucy felt light as a hot-air balloon …up and away. Lucy and Mona parcel as a pair against a wall in the corner on the floor, settling easily into a small space.

The familiar wail of a whistle signals the clickety-clack increasing speed and propeling the troops faster and faster on the rails. Doors weigh wide to scan the scene like a quickening visual quay (or for firing a shot at Rebel bands as need be), while whipping along the way. Clipping cross country at a thoroughbred racer's pace is not a trip Lucy dreamed she would take. Feelings from freedom's elation overwhelm on her face, a bit like when she first got betrothed, started to grow as a grin within, warming like an ever present flame.

Although arriving cheerless and bland within, the boxcar begs many of the men to snooze in relative comfort or just lean in a daze. In relative relaxation others write letters along the way. Lucy perseverates in peace through the ride as well, swaying like an infant rocking in a cradle. She looks downward, casting a glow from a warm, sunny smile you'd save in a frame. Mona dozes in and out nuzzled up to Mama who gently pets her little piglet tails. Casually, she wet her fingers to twirl a stray strand and tuck it back into a tiny mop head braid. Expression expands with no need to speak, just basking in blessings of the present at this time and place. Commitment to grace gushes in her countenance for a Providence purposed path, flushing cerise-cherry blush high on the apples of her cheeks, a look of hope shared in a Mona Lisa maturity exhilarating her face.

Hitherto, but not today, heading to Iuka, (or anywhere in Mississippi for that matter) pushes a past, obdurate fear of abandonment choking throat-high from an inward manacle of shame and still shackling freedom in a silenced cry. Outside the ruddy boxcar, bunchy hills roll far and nigh as variously shaped bluffs briefly become passersby. They approach and then recede through rocks, grass and panoramic pines, styled in stupendous presentation, brightened exceedingly from an earlier sprinkling at first light. The moist-spattered greenery bids hello and goodbye with glistening contrast against a stark, blue sky. Earthy smells blend a fleeting freshness atop the gamey blend of war's odor standing nearby. Lucy breathes in a deep knowing calm that her brave change in life polarizes. Fear and canard promptings of insecurity now belied. They continue to ride.

Pulling her child a little closer in a motherly, cross-armed embrace, she snuggles her richest treasure more tightly asleep at her side. Unpleasant memories surface of the south in her heart, but she kisses Mona's sleepy, nappy head and remains unwavering on the outside. Fetters of the conventional world turn sullen and grave, but Lucy feels free from them in her soul and mind. She has become part of something bigger, pivotal to the point when the guards gave her and Mona refuge and allowed her to work toward preservation of a Union on the Federalist's side.

Incidental to fact, she has no idea where the Chairs chose to remove down the Mississippi line or, if Albert would tackle a case against the Union, when it comes to light. His letter insists a claim on property's pretension, two of them as slaves, by law if it is still his right. Is this something for which the Chairs are willing to spend money on and tussle for in a legal fight? She elects a new motto, 'Out of sight, out of mind.' War's responsibilities give her too much to think and pray about as it is at this time.

Above the day welcomes superb, burnished blue, blending fluffy-white cumulonimbus atop blustery, straggling stratus grays. Lucy remembers well her first experience nursing in the field, the desperate charge of men on skirmishing scourges near Iuka in the midst of war's fray. The end of summer picnic-outing feel of the initial march south sings a honeyed entertainment, slightly soured by the bitter reality over the rise, a solemn, life-threatening phase. It seems the men can turn to "soldier stance" in an instant, but the nurse in "Aunt Lucy" has to learn an adjustment within for triage, so the grueling horrors of blood, ghastly groans of pain and the men's anguished mangling deaths do not take her to task, when maimed. To remain mentally focused through each battle as a nurse and as a mother Lucy undergoes an accelerated, survivalist change. Par to the task, she cuts off woolen, blood clotted clothes, pours water on weltering wounds and steps up to bandage and administer aid like an ace, whilst still keeping an eye on her little one all by the end of that first tedious day.

"Muh havuhsack be filled t'ovuhflowin' wif 'cout'rments o'wahr fo' nuhrsin' an' d'like. We's packin' a newly shahrpen't knife, cotton gauze an' a flask fo' a nip t'ease d'woun'ed pain o'plight, in case a sorry soul's in d'suhr'ous grasp o'death wif dat far away over glazin' look in der eyes. I be standin' wif d'good Chaplain an' Mo' chaffin' at d'bit neah d'bif'ouac off t'de sides. Ohrduhrs t'action: Roguhs gonna carry 'em back, I's gonna clean 'n' ban'age, an' Mo' gonna fill up canteens from a swolled up streamrunnin' back 'n' fawrf as need be, 'bout a rod out muh watchin' sight. Although she be headin' on puhrt neahr fawr o'fi', yuh know she still jus' a lil tyke.

"T'hawrse, Chaplin Roguhs be sittin' wif his head down aprayin' his appeal fo' strength, valuh, an' d'Lawd's savin' light. We's waitin' fo' wuhrd from d'connaissance pattyrolluhs b'fo' he gonna rip reins an' take assistin' flight. Doctuhs back in d'hospituh tents be waitin' wif awll three Stew'rds name' Willy, settin' up fo' d'soljahs mighty ingress. We awll gonna git a pahrt in dis heah fight. A passel o'sojahs be eas'wuhrd five o'six mile', jus' b'f' night. Gath'rin' dahrk come up t'shaduh sev'ruh skuhrmishin', Feduhruh picket rows 'n' g'rilla groups tow'rd Iuka jus' nigh."

"I's a Nuhrvous Nellie, plumb scare't, not fully prepare't fo' d'raucous ruckus o'mil'tary dahrtin' in retreat on d'sly. Nawway's I ready fo' deaf'nin', murd'rous musk'try spen' t'fly. I be mo' like a fat-tailed cat shock't in muh shoes, when d'cracks o'shell 'n' shot knock me shiv'rin' shied. Mo' don' seem t'notice nuffin', jus' happy t'be alive ... dis mos'ly bein' huh only way o'life. Wif me waitin', watchin' tow'rd d'rumblin' thunduh be Mo' standin' wif thumbs poke't up high unduh d'canteen straps jus' right. Pommuh't on huh sho'duhs, slung like suspenduhs fo' trousuhs, dey be hangin' on each side. I know dis heah's a suhr'uhs case o'bidness we's 'bout t'ply, but she look't at me wif huh big ole smile an' I jus' 'bout bus' a gut in delight, laughin' at huh sight."

September and October saw a series of sojourns in segue between skirmishing marches of this nature, contantly on the go. Soon, they head north by foot back to Bolivar and the Hatchie River's flow. They trudge throughout the south two weeks later and yet again they trek back toward their familiar, Bolivar's headquartered home. Marveling at the lengthy, magnificent marches without complaint Mama Lucy and Mona keep up as best they can, wherever the troops might go. They steer their best bravely, failing shoes to blister and eventually callous over, behind the ambulance and supply wagon they move kind of slow. Richie Hollis drives the team of horses, the regular, Wagon Master Host. Sometimes he allows Mona up onto the wagon and lets her hitch a lift for a portion on the road.

Lucy has no expectations for what each day brings, but as far as she is concerned, apart from caring for her young child and the soldiers, she hasn't the need to know. As to all those who are willing to die to help her family live free, she feels they deserve her all, 'til its time to give up the ghost. Nursing duties suit her like being a mother, encompassing the nurturing and maternal spirit of her heart and fulfilling a purpose on the whole.

"Whethuh we's in a lahrge wahrd occuhpyin' d'entahre chuhrch in Bol'var or open in d'fields wif a blazin' battuh seizin' souls in session, I can sho'ly think o'no othuh way fo' Prov'dence t'use me, but in dis honuhbuh profession o'choice."

WANING RESOLVE

For more than a year now, sides for allies and enemies in dispute were chosen, 'Yanks to vie Secesh'. Atavistic anger pilots artillery, confidence to attest. Mortar flames skewer like dragon's breath. Metal necks spew forth fiery arrows and belch smoky, lava-red gases. Careening skyward, the sulfurous sprays spread a hazy shroud, populating the understory in an awful fog of vilipendence. Our nation unfurled battle's fearful dispensation like a scroll to providence.

But for an odd respite after the smoldering stings, clouds climbed quietly and revisited the struggle condensed. Forgiving moisture danced back to the battle as tears from heaven. Was the double dose of precipitation meant to validate or possibly, somehow cleanse? Cannonading hurtles again, chaotic through a thick confusion of orders vibrating amidst deafening shell and brazen, blasting muskets. Sights and sounds muffle in the din ringing in ears to further numb senses. Most of the marshy swamps and rivers swell to overflowing; a wet blanket covering roads and skulking under bridges. Familiar landmarks are submerged, hiding as well in hopes to hear or see no evil intent. Soon the area will be impassable, if unceasing fat droplets continue their kerplopping mud-spatter, sadly dim assurance of further harassment.

To what resolve endless, schlepping marches beneath the battering buckets of tempests do weaken. A cause for restrain at crossings is believed too dangerous to risk wagons and animals or delay soldiers and supplies, yet while soaking downpours drench onward they went. Footsore fighters tromp tired, staggering and bent. The once hale and hearty are now poorly and spent. Miles burn behind them in trespass to sport rag wrapped or bare pegs torn and rent. Unrelenting they trudge mile on trammeled mile of terrain and acreage fenced. At each looping clearance patriotic enthusiasm, once emanating virile energy, wanes against the original and distillating objective, hope of reuniting the states of the Union, repentance confessed. The year's first, intense desire is decreed solicitous at thousands and thousands of soldiers' expense.

Fully south, miles to march remain slimy. An imposition by two and twenty knocks them flat and the thoroughfare, impassable dry shod or clean even in parts, quite the impediment of oozing wet mud to tally. Mucking brick-mortar's sludge and its colleague, mortarshocking shards, mix among the rotting autumn leaves. Obstacles add expression to injury's endurance indelibly. Dead, embattled men and horses, ruined wagon wheels, artillery fragments and accoutrement pieces portray a macabre amalgamation for all to see. The resultant collage from three previous battles fought at this destination cannot keep a secret and deeply scar the disastrous scene. Divergent outcroppings, ruts of entrenchments bare boots sadly sucked down unforgiving and weary, notched to the knee. Emotions mix melancholia, double-minded with mud, accompaniments' increase to exhaustion and darken spirits of every soldier begging they camp alee.

Patches of color that draw the eye to autumn's awe and appeal, the richly hued russet and sunstruck gold, bold and brassy beside burnt-ochre, edged by coppery browns on lush pinnate leaves, now tramples under feet. Likely God chose to finish His fertile portrait early, endorsing death's propinquity. Never to be known negligent in His seasonal response to rendering bare the bulging trees, but dulling sadness ripens to rot with the year's preceding gravity. Nature's costume is nearly bleak, but many, the ungrateful, are distracted in the mean. The display gives no one favor to plead for reprieve, when ceasing to find God's glory in humanity. No soul here sits in leisure savoring bursts of beauty from a porch parceled freely sipping a relaxing cup of tea. War's phenomenon speaks environmentally, allegorically, and dismally as God's witness to our disabled country's purpose deviate on a castigating, sparring spree. Bar the honored, humbled souls longing, nay begging to be free.

"When I looks on d'sky, drizzlin' rain come t'splash muh stuck out tongue an' wash muh uptuhrned face, whils' Mo' lay nappin', hunkuhr't down in d'wagon's cawrnuh wif a rubbuh blanket, a harmless space. Ev'n though we's in de fawrcibuh bidness o'deadly war, I be lookin' o'er d'Lawd's lan' an' I cain't hep but fas'nate on d'seasons' changin' grace. D'King o'Kings choose' His timely aim t'paint coluhrs 'n' good fawrtune on d'whole o'de country, but I knows He showed He can jus' as easy take it away. Thusly, we's stahrtin' t'think ahr hopes fo' a quick'nin' en' t'dis heah wahr beginnin' t'sink 'n' bluhr below a puhrfec' wat'ry bog an' fade."

Exuberance and endurance peak a couple of months into the fall of '63 with overzealous ideas for a quickened finale. Time gapes wounds of war too, America bleeds Legions limp, more lassitude and weak into wintrier weather, whilst terrible shells sneeze like banshees shriek. Two armies battled first and second across the farther southern fields. Horror whacks us hard in the heart, catching us fifty miles off guard upon reach. Shell shattered structural sections are sunken, submerged half deep. Oddly fossilized in pinnalcled parts and covered with crusted mud and blood, folks and carnage litters the field. Barely recognizable between the stench and weird imprints, clothes, and gear are haphazardly strewn hither and yon emaciating in bloated putrefaction and partially rise from the dirt unceremoniously.

Though some lay completely unseated, affected by the season's meanest degrees, we could glean snapshot fragments of battles we hadn't seen, cryptic clues to swashbuckling phantoms and advancing infantry. Shocking most in bothersome disarray were interments partially breached. Unfortunate, previous burials unreasonably set them free. Burial plots were dug hastily for naught it seems. An interminable rain mustered out the martyred men in soiled, blue coats from their earthen beds stained brownish and burgundy-green. As if mud maintains their clothes in native element, coats and trousers refuse the clean. Nights honor the chill with a medal of frozen feet. Shoes soggy from slogging crust with a circumference of musty, mother earth embracing them in a moistened ring. Rubber blankets bring no relief.

The Western Theatre continues to toil troops, driving them back and forth into the swampy, southern states deeply. By winter's solstice penurious provisions are scarce as hen's teeth. All that is left of their original rations are hard, moldy cracker bits to eat. They rummage around for stale cornpone and handfuls of field beans with weak coffee. The animals they might have foraged are hibernating, tunneled deep in burrows to sleep. On the other hand, the soldiers have had little to no sleep on the freezing cold ground with blankets thinning like their waistlines, quite lean, neither proper uniforms in cheap supply nor shoes, which beg repair's need. Ingredients in this recipe of war whip feelings, once cheery into spirits darkly stirred and dank as the region laid waste and destitute by war's consequential seal. God bless America's aim through the tumultuous and deadly devastation to heighten a hope of the later, greater victory.

"Miss'sip' wintuh mud whar now col' an' rock hahrd, in ridges 'n' gullies from d'tawrrents afta d'las' battuhs on d'field, trump't up like tree stumps in a hahrd row dat cain't take d'seed. D'weathuh done check't us drea'fuh complete. Awll d'folks Nawrth t'Souf, Union t'Rebs, take on d'mannuh o'downtrodden souls, tossed, ailin', an' deprived o'sleep. A stragglin' on blistuh't feet see'd mos' dis'pline fawrgot', a sad state o'mil'tary beggin' God's muhrcy fo' suhrvivuh needs…well, mos' neahrly."

➤⟋⟍➤

Rose buds open ajar on the window, vibrant crimson and vermillion colors in good stead. Soon, they wilt and petals begin to droop and fall away, brown and dead. I think about this process and realize her regiment is overwhelmed with epidemic illness away from healthy food, lack of shoes and awkward odds toward aseptic defense. Pangs of homesickness gnaw at the gut away from family, hearth, and those who love you best. Similar to the Army of the Potomac, feelings of patriotic dread spread with the trauma of war like an epidmic disease, without hope to soon be on the mend. American economy, the self-created creature, is put to a willful test.

"I membuhs miasma'd mis'ry floatin' on d'bittuh win's prevailin'. Decayin' men 'n' hawrses be uncovuh't from shalluh graves. D'blame goin' t'fawll like ahr constan' companion d'rain. Some soljahs be suff'rin' from infections o'woun's pain. Ev'n a whiff o'whiskey ain't gonna heal dat kinda ailin'. Muh own appetite fo' faith be stahrtin' t'ache dishahrt'n, hongry an' failin'. Sickness 'n' death disahrm mos' folks' prej'dice, still at odds wif wahr's grotesque brutal'ty availin'."

"By d'las' days o'autumn leaves cahrpeted de groun' yelluh 'n' buhrgun'y red. Dat ole foe Miss'sip', 'bout t'see me white as a sheet in a buhrnin' bed. D'Ahrmy o'Tenn'see ready t'stan' down fo' a spell, seein' as deys nothin' but dearth 'n' death, ev'n fo' us folks dat still got great numbuhrs left. God say dat hap'n fo' a reason I specs. Spir't done shrink from puhrpose 'n' sacr'fice, so quick t'fawrgit. Dis heah lan' o'blood, ash, 'n' snow mix't wif emotion, set in a mahrtyrs mol', d'fine whut folks gonna do wif d'life d'Good Lawd gif 'em nex'."

"Uhrly dat nex' yeahr, folks begin t'suffuh d'likes o'skeettuh-fevuhs, swamp-sickness, ague mis'ry, meezuhs, dysynt'ry, Typhoid an' sich t'check. We be mo' like a mahrchin' hospituh, mos' folks stem t'stuhrn be a wreck. It be tol', ahrmies mahrch on dey bellies, but we's so footso' n' blistuh't, we's disin'gratin' wif no en'rgy t'fight an' ready t'crawl on awll fo's, jus' dragglin' t'base camp beggin' t'heck wif d'whole mess. 'Cause ev'n though d'Good Pres'den' Lincoln brung slaves from freedom t'success, but d'Souf ain't 'bout t'regress. Soljuhs down dere still defendin' got barely enough eats t'keep a skeeta's wings flappin' in d'stress. If'n a strong bafflin' win' whar t'commence, d'whole lotta Rebuh laggahrds be blow'd off d'lan' t'a new address. D'season's end done made us weak as dandylions blowin' out on a chile's whim 'n' wish, but by God's Grace defeat ain't nuffin' we wonts t'accept."

Forget regret of war, the repentant defenders survive fallow fields, frosty days and biting cold nights somehow without recant. Refurbishment finally arrives on repaired rails, although the quantity is a might scant. Some fresh food is handed out, as well as black boots and a spotless shirt for each man needing to be reclad. Pork and hardtack come toward January's end, as well as a respite from the wretchedly relentless, skirmishing rants. The experiences mature, but age one as well, a wrinkling to expressions around the eyes is warranted. Hair too, straggles gray by the temples and the weather drys and cracks the hands. Battle fatigue and homesick pangs bring the merriest soul to a bluish-gray, often appearing sunken in the eyes and gaunt or deadpan.

Regimental faith, nonetheless resolute, pushes steadfast to a precipitant, onerous variance. Ramshackle warriors finally receive a welcome grant. A breath of relief comes from the bitter marches and field camps. At capacity, though limited by mileage on rails, the train accommodates as grateful a rest as the Sabbath for a span. Almost purring as they sway, an end to inadequate sleep, the boxcars pacify fast. The movement hypnotizes like a magically floating pendulus timepiece to lull each man into a silent trance. They suggestively arrest their eyes and pathetically roughshod feet, even for those who must stand. Thankfully grace renders the weather by the time the troops breach Bolivar's base camp.

Lucy, a few wives, stewards, doctors and Pastor Rogers, those with hospitable leanings, spring into action and tend to the men. Though they are not finished with the war, the troops begin to revalidate inside and out as to their purpose in fighting the Rebs. Some make vain attempts to wash out the negativity and cynicism from dirty, matted and mentally decimated heads. Plenty of lye soap and clean water is put goodly to use and scours months of scum, pain and battles' regret. Hygiene and medicine in earnest begin to heal physically, and so new uniforms, accoutrements and drills encourage patriotic demeanor back in good stead.

Tender branches snap for kindling as crackling bonfires roars beneath big black, stew kettles. Fresh rations keep rumbling stomachs fed, while eventual balance spiritually is entertained by letters and packages from warm homefires, which they've been longing for and fitfully dreaming about in nights on some makeshift bed. Sleep comes in the stationary base camp for now on familiar soil in familiar buildings with beds or cots and dry, rubber blankets. All the former tests prepare the 23rd infantry in diligent fashion with a humbling experience. They will need every, burnished bit as they practice through spring months for Vicksburg… their greatest test of faith yet.

WRESTLING
WITH ANGELS

On Christmas of 1862 the regiment returns to Tennessee, after trying to reach Vicksburg, hitherto attempted and failed twice and put to rest. They camped to reevaluate in an old field about twelve miles south of Oxford without pay or rations, dependent solely on the land and God's hand for subsistence. Extraordinarily cold in Colliersville this Eve; substantial snow's thaw and freeze obstructed the roads ordinarily accessible on the long sojourns and at times insufferable to some extent. Matters all the worse, less became less, once soldiers were eight months on with nonexistent wages intervening, conceivably "unavoidable circumstances", but more notably, unprepared, inexcusable and inefficient.

"Pastuh Roguhs be chahrgin' inta suhrmons 'n' prayuh meetin's 'gahrdless o'de inclemen' whethuh or in d'face o'many men feahrin' d'en'. He sho nuff summon jus' d'right wuhrds t'glue d'fawrces o'faith stuck at a dead en' back t'gethuh an' git us through patches dat's roughes', no mattuh whar, no mattuh when."

Soldiers' respect for their Chaplain improves in favor through his bountiful religious zeal, which heightens morale, impossible at times to materialize or maintain. Benefits of spiritual support do sustain; gives a crutch to one's hobbling will, during war and pain. God sees The Grim Reaper at the ready and the death toll off the chain. Quite the misunderstood phenomenon, the heart and spirit may be quantifed or described, but never adequately by statistics and dates. Journalists' reports as well cannot fully express emotions to words in a newsy way, when alluding to an enlightened soldier's letter made plain.

Tantamount to testimony, sentiment openly professed in prayer more often governs grace, vulnerablility in witness best expressed to His face. When involvement in traumatic trials pervade past surviving limits, people are moved to extend emotion, beyond the feigning and external appearance of skin shades to penetrate genetic's casting grade. Miracles mingle with an unrelenting will as we begged for life on this unforgiving, mortal plain. Inconceivable tragedies, often horrific and harrowing, as well as mystifying alternatives mankind may make, bring sense into being in black and white, though we attempt, but can't explain away the shades of gray.

Periodic revivals boost the company's morale throughout each week, the Holy Spirit's climate saturates. Bonds of brothers rebuild and renew in strength through faith, which may be the only thing that mitigates the multiple demoralizing tragedies a soldier continues to sustain. Four scores of men read their Bibles daily as possible and stir up gratitude for life lived to the maximum, a tenable purpose from God's saving grace. They increase knowledge of scripture to thwart hardships and the basest, brutish carnage they have seen in their lives to date.

Lucy and Mona are never taught to read a page, so upon hearing, they listen everso intently with ears hanging on Chaplain Rogers' every word with supreme, praise. Their incandescent eyes riveted equally …captivated.

"Know this about war in every instance of our earthly flesh." rich tones preach conviction and resonate like a spartan warrior beating his breast, "In this instant peace in your heart does exist, to the extent that no impending perilous fear can squelch, of when or how your life's spirit will be spent." Chaplin Rogers questions to chasten, directly dissecting the essential impetus for the soul's offense, "Do you wrestle with your choice, still in defense of sins, like Jacob with the angel? …I say, now. *Make amends*! Do not leave this country, whether it thrives or struggles, clothed in sins to offend. If the gross imbalance is not stifled and redressed, we will bear the sins of our fathers upon our children's children, yet uncleansed. Realize your cup can not fill with faith and fear alike in intent. Fear drains as dehydration, never allowing the soul's thirst to be quenched. Courageously claim your allegiance in faith to a cup always overflowing. *Recognize Omniscience*."

"Even if a single day's fight transpires to lengthen into many and an angry, blood-soaked moon hastens a ring of red, let neither an intemperate cold, nor manna's lack, nay death's grim devastation languishing the land fill your vulnerable heart with dread. When His encompassing care blankets your spirit bed, regardless of circumstance, God's love rules and will not rest. *God is wide awake on the Throne of Heaven*. Open your eyes! Be impressed! Remember the Good Book fills the centuries with wars' saving scripts made by ordinary men. You too can take up that cross in this our nation's story, which will be written for generations to read, learn and harken. For surely as we may die today or extend the tale to tell, the Union's strength is the stuff of legends."

While Chaplain's miraculous message of inspiration, Providence led, penetrates into each soul's essence, his breath shoots out in heated fervency, condensing. "Make no mistake; if you are still here and have not breathed your last breath, your purpose in His victory has not seen its final recompense. I say to the Rebels, do your worst, for we shall do our best! Stand fast as Job in this permissible test. If He has not yet taken your life and called you to your heavenly home, let Him take your feet swiftly and rally thence to the next bend. Beg for strength from His omnipotence. Hear me now and fully listen, The Almighty has no need to raid the rail from a fence, tender fires to boil coffee and beg the break to rest my brave friends!"

The bedraggled bits of the Tennessee's regiment lingered amidst freezing chills and windswept winter's silence. "Den we grin 'n' nod, 'cause dat's jus' what we be doin'... right den. Awll d'men takes a quick'nin' glance 'roun', one t'nothuh an' lift up dey cup, dey fists 'n' long muskets in a shout, 'AMEN!...AMEN!' We guh'ps d'las' bit o'wahrmin' coffee, scuttuhs d'fahres wif duhrt an' gits goin' on d'road agin singin' a mahrchin' type, fife 'n' drum hymn."

The compelling account sends healing to me trebly, bringing forth the anguish of privacies' in confessional. There is no matter this is Lucy Higgs' witness of Pastor

Rogers to a third party's telling. I stare at the sage truth in her eyes and fight tears' indulgence, a knowing peace swells with a growing inner welling. Shame-sullied decades of shadows beg forgiveness. Please hear my soliliquy as witness to my repentance, a humblest retelling.

"There are days in war's beginning I signify tempestuous skies like the whole of Heaven's angels crying awash of tears across castigated souls, if I speak allegorically. I'm mishmashing within me the sense of a soldier's barbaric killing sprees as purposed compelling. Each encounter wages uglier than the last with precipitous hours of death's dismay inbetween, during and after, melancholy begins indwelling. My apathy grows hollower still. I no longer battle across fields as an insect devours the fields. Emptiness has left me feeling more like the cast off locust shell. Prayers to the heavens for earthly battles to be victorious burn raw on my knees, but there is no surrendering and few conflicts to relish. My comrade's deaths remain afresh, a tableau I'm unable to erase and torturously undispelling."

"Why did the trials of this life not become mercy and spiritual growth in disguise for me with angels singing praises for God's reveling? Battles we fight eventually quell, but impenetrably buried beneath my compatriots in arms, tenets of truth absolute ring like a cracked bell. Hope shatters mid-field in powdery, blackening blasts and a deafening shelling. What first I saw as loyalty to God and country with a quickening, military end, exploded as anger, sending me in pieces to a public, and yet profoundly private, hell within. All those rainbow dreams of adventure and the vital patriotic verve of the waving flag flatly fell in my heart, even before I could begin to sell it to myself."

"Blue, white and red cover brethren in blood, my cousin as well as childhood friends. I gave my word to his mother, my Aunt Nelly. I had sworn to protect this junior drummer, not yet to his life's summer, spent at the tender age of twelve. On some bastard field, undeserving and barren, I closed my cousin's eyes, so thoughtful and affectively susceptible. I no longer bought what the war was selling. How coould I face his mother with the lifeless body of her son or even send the post to tell of it? Confusing thoughts bloat the emptiness like a miasma of unanswered questions within my heart and nauseate like rancid pork in my belly."

"That first winter at war I must sigh to expel, lest I forget with the incompetent ramblings of age to my own undoing and all too well. Christmas cracks me like an all too fragile eggshell. All around us one morn upon return from picket, a Godsent gift, the whitest snow, pure and undriven, for hours fell. Strewn fluffy and bristling crisp in the twilight air upon dozens of hewn timber stumps from logs we'd been felling, circular downy drifts float atop, while troops are asleep inside winter dwellings. The remnant stubs resemble tables with cloths whitened in blueing, but the moon's glowing hue brings a sheen that is shimmering. Readily romantic for a fluted, flowering vase, claret wine, cheddar cheese and a flirty, story's telling."

"The subzero night froze extremities, the loneliest picket vigil to be. Supplies of shoes and socks deny the feet longer than my exhausted army's pay, now deplete. Some of my toes exemplify the deportment of eggplants with purplish, blue-black edges blistering in throbbing pain up to the balls of my feet, fat and swelling. Desire to see my family, frantic doubts of making it to the end, even surviving the season at all, press in as a tightening vice or throng enveloping. Embittered tears inundate hot wetness on my cold cheeks like the dam gone weak cracks to flood a flush of debris down mainstreet. Left to my own reflection unremedied, fear falls in pieces like a looking glass of hope smashing to smithereens. Quicksilver slivers of defeatism drip down over the prior world perceived. In a jarring agony I forget Jesus would see all and can well repair this nation, the world …or me".

"Victimizing my shame I whimper a most piteous groan and yell, 'Why?' Drowning in remorse and drivel I decide I had made a monumental mistake choosing this living hell. Inward shudders hold onto war's regret, while splashy drops pool a peculiar profile quietly wept. The rubbery bedroll grows sodden, ignominious an repelling. To my knowledge everyone else sleeps well, but the heaviest of hoary snows and the hardness of my heart like a measuring stone fell."

"I cannot curse Him, but, instead make the weightiest wager, God in all His sovereignty becomes a stranger. I suffer to find a mustard seed of faith in its tinest splinter. A weeper positioned like a fetal infant, I curl and tremble at the bottom of despair's pit and wallow darkened. Estrangement from my mortal sins overwhelms my berth. In a self-made, bereft cavern I lay feeling cursed, rejecting a single note's hum for a hymn, even whispered. Not one refrain sung; neither from Christmas carols, nor in recounting the glory of Jesus' birth. No rendering remembrance stirs with even the simplest sentence heard. I implore you as heretofore, unable to release the disquieting indwelling, I survive, now dumbfounded and flustered."

My eyes open to gape down at the elderly, weathered porch planks greatly effaced. Straight realization abruptly bumps me to attention slightly ashamed. The bane of contention made plain wrings my hands inveighed. Lucy lengthens from her rocker's stance, wizened hands heavily position atop mine with fingers splaying to fasten an embrace. I watch her wrinkled knuckles, russet raisins so prayerfully laid, and I'm able to breathe and holster the shakes. Subsequently, shallower exhale trails unload the cumbersome freight. A curtly nod follows to handle my tighter façade finally braced.

She squeezes atop my hands, pats them twice and nods agreeance, "Mmhm," very slow and low in a comforting way, saying, "God unduhstan's awll ahr pain, ev'n d'kind we cain't esplain. S'pose dat's anuthuh thin' ain't gonna make sense 'til d'Judgemen' Day. No mattuh whuht done happen, it gonna be okay. Ev'n in d'groanin' hahrt, God gonna gitcha through d'roughest swamps 'n' watuhways. He heahrs d'mos' broken pray. He knows wahrs is drea'fuh…jus' drea'fuh dispar'gin', no mattuh how d'endin' gonna play."

She shifts in her seat with an endeavoring sway, smiling the warm truth born of a sage. Enough encouragement enters my heart to look up and breathe anew the day, while I wipe a trickling tear streak born for the young boy's sake. Indeed, I swear the feisty sky just took on a deeper hue against the landscape. For each of the men fortunate to be under her care during the war, she must have rendered the same grace. I shall not deny why Providence, miraculous in mercy, has led me to this humbling place...or employed Lucy through Civil War's campaign, still healing soldiers in His holy name.

IMPASSIONED VIGILANCE

Atop a willowy branch of lilting, leafy tendrils, two yellow warblers whistle and preen. Their melodic trills twitter sweetly before they flit to the canopy's retreat. Hidden within the upper branches, they flirt lyrically between fattening feasts of juicy caterpillars and sundry, insects' increase. Subtle sounds of spring summarily awake a few, groggy recruits with new equipage before the rest of the regiment begins details' replete. Their titillating twitters nudge a few from yawning's keep. Some still draw scabbards to slash and parry in dreamy, heroic duels, while other wayward sleepers wrestle with nightmares, screaming about grisly, distressing scenes.

Dawn's creamy linen nonetheless sheds its cloudy nightshirt to expose war in stark-naked reality. Incubus or reverie releases them as kinsmen, rough and ready. If not roused with speed, soldiers felt their cots yanked out from beneath. Any carousers considering wayward siestas still assemble bug-eyed and ruddy after tasting a pail of chilly water shucked on their face from Sergeant Robert Cazee. General Sanderson's infantry didn't usually receive this sort of reprimand though, not even a slap upon the cheeks. They tumbled out of tents in uniform spectacle to the bellowing, embouchured bray of a buglar's blare and the drummer boy's cadent beats.

April, 1863, the ever lucid banner of stars and stripes flutters steadily, flying amast on a bountiful breeze. Below the vast footprint of a base camp monitors Memphis, Tennessee. Lassitude no longer, Indiana's 23rd infantry recuperates smartly; a bleak abeyance the dreary winter had seen. Carefully, spiritual capitulation for God's gifts, country, and cause soon converts the soldiers' creed drive to an inroad bonding robust and healthy. Indeed needed, if they strive toward the finish in victory. Hope's healing reveals in due season, consoling as spring's emerald colored, baby buds espied newly. In the mean, infantry fit to survive battle's bleed reassemble schema thusly, in hopes they endure to the end without going round the bend, deserting in fear, shame or apathy or cowering like scared felines up the proverbial tree. These men groom grit from the gut like surgery without chloroform or whiskey. They strengthen character like seasoned outlaw deputies or vigiliantes, now no longer green.

Although not yet weighed, measured, or obligatory, realization of triumph exists vaguely in the patriotic heart to cosset coming honor and glory. Within the soul struggling for earthly endurance, polished medals are reserved for the hour we celebrate or grieve and at least in some semblance heal to enjoy war's zeal. With just a badge bowdlerized of bravery soldiers laid siege with vigilance and daring, par to defend again like the ancient hero's protagonist Hercules or Achilles. Feeble heels loom timorous, but we invite invincibilty in theory. Does this not intimidate and beg our country's comrades, if not to surrender, fall and bleed? Trepidation's battle breeds atVicksburg, the next target city.

—◢▮◣—

Lucy entwines her fingers with a grin and clasps them tightly together, inside her palms like the children's church rhyme without the steeple, wiggling within.

"Dey pack us like sahrdines, crowdin' onta ships wif steel keels. I be heahrin'wuhrd Gen'ral Gran'gots anuthuh trick up his sleeve, strat'jizin' amids' d'wahr's din 'n' plannin' a gran', shebangin' siege. We wonts t'stick wif 'im through d'strikin' blockade an' d'nex' steps t'vict'ry. Dat big ole padduh be wheezin' big billuhs o'stawrmy, gray steam. If'n you please, how can yuh not be incline' t'be pahrt o'dat pow'ful feel?"

To squelch this coveted, commanding fortification, which crowns the peak above a Mississippi knoll, demands a diverse strategy. General Grant is peeved to eccentric puzzling. Vexing, irreversable losses of souls, supplies and opportunities, thus far, foil his pivotal ploy to 'pocket the key'. Although we tore them thrice engaged to just within reach, the challenge to checkmate does not come with ease. A backlash, which sorely boomerangs, crushes hope for a Union lead. Slave gangs, eager in emancipation excavate a channel to change the flow of the Mississippi, infringing further upon the citadel, but no deal. Daily burials in shallow graves are sown in haste along the unfortunate shore, revealed just as quickly by the broken and eroding, washed out levees. The days are disheartening, undeniably.

His reconfiguration blueprint is the inroad to success, but the triumph brought to tell is bittersweet. General

Grant amasses an army almost forty thousand strong; soldiers march and maneuver around Vicksburg from states afar, sheltering alee. The closing circle elongates the outcome however, vital in this siege. Astride his beautiful, bay mare, a man of vigilance, cigars and fixed principles, rides through opposition's attack, which seethes, not only from Vicksburg's grand, stronghold of artillery, but as well from his impatient and intemperate colleagues. They rustle frustrated, up and around the mighty Mississippi, on to the east, two thousand miles away in Washington, D. C. that do not agree. (This angst, of course, included General Halleck's negative, discrediting pleas.) In chambers President Lincoln, notwithstanding concerns of others to relegate, remains in good favor of Grant's predictable perseverance and fearless frontline fighting abilities, which are sorely needed.

War's violence escalates to vitriolic reeling, a whirling dervish akin to an agile mongoose striking a coiled King Cobra repeatedly. Odds given to win, but the toll mounts grim at the inception as unremoved corpses pile an effluvium, polluting putrid in stench from exposure to heat. Pemberton decrees an initial armistice dispatching from inside the walled city. Spades and shovels raise and arms lower to drag wounded to safety, warily trade coffee (truly) and bury dead in shallow earthen embankments, humanity's last ditch effort of Christian sanity. (Wounded had been begging for water and hope of healing for hours entrenched in those ravines.) An eerie, quiet echo consumes the redans and rolling fields between tossed dirt and countless, inarticulate voices murmuring prayers and pleas, not quite to the hour of three. With an ordered waving motion the white flags tuck away and heed business as usual, war's arduous creed. The respite of truce was, nonetheless, not meant to tease or trumping favor, thus more soldiers fall and the wounded remuneration of consequence increases.

By April of '63, the Union's intrepid man of methods counters a brilliant strategy, passive-aggressive. Shortly, a calvalcade invasion will unleash. Staunch General Sherman reinforces Grant north of his aim, bluff replete. Initially amphibious in nature, the adaptation occurs under a cloud of cigar smoke, while studying maps strewn across his desk for weeks. The arched offensive of joint, army-navy, cooperation continues culminating an operation of retribution's defeat. Twelve barges bulging with troops, stores and intention set afloat the darkened, muggy waters at full throttle speed. Largely they navigate the centerline of alternating strips, water and lowlands, winding circuitously. Our soldiers and supplies include a band's introduction aboard the Benton, tailing serpentine in the flotilla down river, surprisingly with relatively few casualties.

The traversing river is set fire on each shore by southern rebels to light up the silent, soldiering majority on barges in the dank darkness as targets for all to see. Cotton bales soak in turpentine aflame with a blackened sheen, riverside residences blaze as torches and barrels of tar light an interminable, shore's edge bonfire buoyed by the spring's river breeze. Confederate objective completely outlines us against the black for all to see. Embarking on a clandestine ticket aboard the steamer is now aglow betwixst flaming, orange-red gleams. Veteran navigators, tough and spitting nails, not only as warriors, but as the gunboat team are what the Union need. The original crews refuse to venture a voyage with so many vessels to the hazard, daunted as well by possible exploding, unprotected batteries. Shot or shell upon passenger ships was perceived martyrdom as the bulkhead would not shield.

Albeit an arbitrary plan, Indiana's 23rd does not flinch and faces the enemy with doubled fists, nobly furnishing the "J.W. Chessman" and "Horizon" with volunteer hands of over seventy. General Grant lauds exacting character to their allotted duties. Officer Davis steps up, rallies the fleet's southward run and prevails over the unheard of odds against a hardnosed enemy. The canister blasts, shells (round and grape) shot, tearing the pilot houses away entirely. Lucy and Mona float down river with the band on the Benton's steam.

D'fuhrst leg o'dat juhrney still puhrc'late' like a dream. I ain't nevuh step' boot t'bawrge b'fo' dis eve', but I sees thin's in a lib'ratin' fashion, since I come t'de Union milit'ry. Muh hahrt b'gin t'beat fastuh 'n' fastuh as we move t'racin' speed. Danjuh may be as neah as a sneeze, but I be smellin' d'sweet air o'freedom on d'rivuh's breeze. Mo' be safe, I tucks huhr in d'cawrnuh 'tween muh knees."

They are firing hails of exploding volleys. Succored by the current they successfully carry coal, rations, ordnance stores and hundreds of soldiers to the most southerly port beyond the "Guardian of the Mississippi" to ferry back across and march, northerly and east. The majority survive the dangerous and grisly gauntlet to accomplish the next feat. Once south of the towering fortress, the lot debarks at port on an opposing shore to convey. A maddening march with limited rations impedes. Secesh guerillas rout in retreat toward Vicksburg setting fire to bridges as they flee with the ire of a beast. This strategy demands we build, rebuild and wade knee high to waist deep. Pontoons carry the artillery shells in scorching heat, while the men are driving hard and dripping sweat in pungent, stagnant streams. A longitudinal, obtuse arc sets the divisions in a semicircle to fortify farther north and east.

"Quick as a whippuh snappuh, dem Rebuhs stahrts a fahrin' shell an' shot from d'shawr neahr d'trees. I jus' says t'Mo' dat we needs t'pray dese ships gits us t'whar we's goin' in one piece. In a smawll cawrnuhr we takes a knee. Prayin' souls glean wheat from d'chaff, so, when ill at ease you tame d'wild nuhrves like a jaw breakin' din o'ahrtill'ry spree. Notwifstandin' d'puhrfec' timin' o'Prov'dence, prayin' mos' use'ly bring d'hahrt t'a place o'peace, so we ain't gonna cease."

At the furthest, southern point of ferry, 500 or so slaves crowd around, a boisterous agreeable sort. Their Saturday night jubilee begins as a customary sort without much thought of war to report. Banjos, mirth and a lighthearted humor of song and dance greet our musicians, practically pulling them onto an oppressive shore. Philosophy and pride concerning war's result consort. Ancient as Moses and heaped in tradition they converge, but deeply seated, spiritual praise pours forth. A reeling rendition of "Home Sweet Home" plays by the twenty third's violinists, flautists and a few brasses bringing tears to homesick soldiers coerced by the atmosphere's force. They reassemble and file forward forging an easterly bearing as combatants slog through bogs and get north by way of Raymond past a few ports.

Grant is fast becoming Pemberton's only adversary to untie the river's toughest knot with a cut in the style of Gordian's lore. No burning blaze, battles waged or burning bridge taxing duty's chore is going to pull them off course. Troops persist on foot with only blankets for equipage and no other support, including officers, not one unsuffers to horse. Reconnaissance informs them by sporting the maze of levees and exploratory scouting further inland and ascertains ashore. Some continue on and others remove to the next port. At each point additional orders are given, need to know basis only, on the fly to accord. Eventual thousands arrive from states near and far still loyal to colors and pursuant to each new plan on course.

Skirmishing challenges a setback at Raymond, an unfortunate thirty miles from our final bivouac report. An ambush, hits hard and gores, not considered foolhardy or fireproof, amidst an aim of five Rebel regiments camouflaged in the understory. Swallowed whole in a sucking onslaught kicks us forward, separate from our main corp. Hundreds in the slurry pour shot sent to targets aplenty, trampled sore.

Providence parlays the threat after the worst, mercifully realigning on the other side are survivors. They attach to Illinois' 45th, a Union corps. Fully a hundred plus heroes martyr to a devastated dirt floor, including twenty as prisoners captive in the inane disorder, now inside Vicksburg, our foe's fort. Herald those in harm's way, but not to forget, Hiram Murphy, for his heroism and success rescuing our colors. We head to the rally point, thankfully, without loss of another soldier. Indiana's 23rd holds on tightly and sure till the city surrenders. We joined forces with the 45th for those final forty days to crest the base of the enemy's works.

The conduct of a wetland climate instead gives discomfort proof, more than navigating the peculiars of geography. Swills of swamps swarm with annoying gnats and mosquitoes infest malarial fevers and ague's ails, harsh and mean. Early morning mists too unseen, not only heave and soak shirts and flesh by midday's steam, the sweat sops skin down in streaming sheets from a broiling, blistering mid May heat. Otherwise flourishing and radiant, the picturesque scene is vivd with colors, a thriving understory. Many of the men ogle at fragrant oleanders, vibrant, emerald greens, spicy-scented pepperbushes and the airy clusters of calliopsis, which give an anomalous greeting. Their bi-colored petals burst as rivulets of wine spilling; showy golden and mahogany-merlot petals, most inviting. Luxuriant examples scenting meadows keenly light up their vista, mesmerizing magnolias, most enrapturing, unsteady the senses, when one first smells the odorous treat.

VEHEMENT VENGEANCE

American flags, the red, white and blue anchor. Hither and yon conquering colors fly in gradient slopes apportioned. They meticulously plant within range of rifle-pitted anchors, which the sortie bastions bore. It is their sobering answer of patriotic support. Soldiers of the North lob laborious rounds at the sovereign city on the shore. Days and nights can't keep score and protest to the pace of vectors dashing munitions, which blast at the city's core. Trajectories flash like fireworks in constant fiery stores. While the fallen dead lay as shot on the bloodied, muddy floor, others stampede over them, virulent to the fore. The scene darkens nightly, akin to a repeating stage-death, encore upon gruesome encore. As if the crowd begs for more, additional companys rest to switch out, so another regiment can carry on the fight and kill, or die, if God permits, to reinforce.

Battling with voracity the thirsting and ravenous contenders hunker in earthen works. Dug in like ticks for a score of days affray to court. Unpurged with no ambulance able to remove wounded asunder torn. Badly bleeding, hungering and begging for water…quite the impossibly tall order to assist as rations ordered to be brought must stretch beyond at fifteen days short. Victuals secured in bivouacs beyond the bluff can be scuttled zig-zag ingress and egress, the only possible retort.

Thankfully, canteens satiate with water from a run-off thread by the Glass Bayou fork. The infantry refills and heartily eats beans and fried pork, albeit a makeshift picnic on an unpeaceful shore. Now clean water, unless boiled, is scarce and evaporates like forgotten folklore. Imploring the Holy Spirit, for health and life, as priceless as pearls, and to return home to hearth, prized sacred all the more.

Perpetually pushing Confederates back, General Grant gives command to his men, *'Unmoor!'* unyielding in advance. Sidetrack to Federal's offensive line, some soldiers are singing "Close the Ranks Firmly" like troubadours waxing poetic aft. It actually rallies the warriors' attitudes, during a transitory cessation in combat. Indiana's infantry takes point to attack, immediately engaging and holding positions, front and back. Demanding skills shoot forth zeal intact, like to an oil well uncapped and proving to lionize the patriots' craft.

At Port Gibson other generals laud praise to the legion as 'glorified sons of Indiana, yet unmatched'. Indubitably, it is most unfortunate no interlude is given to throw up celebratory caps or pat each other or ourselves for that matter, on the back. Maneuvering and fighting tactics of this severity endeavor to saddle them awkward, their shoes wear holey and flat. As they retreat Rebels engulf each bridge in a conflagration and demand we gather a muscling detail to patch the damage, which slows our flank. Perseverance powers on by using the retrieved, singed planks.

A month of smoky assaults soars higher, fighting ashore. May's torrents storm as a deluge at death's door, and thusly musket shot sends men to a muddier, bloodier fighting floor. As if a biblical inundation is in store, tears from Heaven respond in demise to the gore. It keeps up strong and sure, all the next day from the night before. Mississippi mud country admonishes indifferent within its core. Comparatively copious with the superb glory of sweet flora and fauna bursting with brighter notes against the oozy muck and slimy mud plastering Louisiana's damp and swampy shore. We are able to advantage fresh rain for water and avail food from dense, lush woods for forage. Assemblages work to survive a long campaign, told to take only as needs be by immediacy and portability from abandoned stores. Uncontrolled farms around the countryside bequeath beef, bacon, mutton, field beans and corn.

Nonetheless worse for wear, jaunty companies sally forth, rapid and diligent in effort with formidable disposition to the fore, such was the multitudinous force of the Army of the Tennesse corps. Indiana's base camp sets far eastside, alternate a large, italic hillock beyond the intersection of Jackson Road where it splits like wood hacked with an axe to the cord. There it veers off onto Countryman Road and advantages left to a full, flush mile of meadow's galore.

Opposite the thoroughfare's south fork, a feminine proprietor, stubborn to evacuate a large white house, is sent packing sore. After three days of housefire tore, she shakes out, whilst her slaves scarper like yelping puppies with cinder-burnt tails rushing out the door. Although they hide by a lanky chimney, they claim Union support. No obstacles to traffic, Indiana's 23rd Infantry travels forth.

Spades and rifle butts in full swing hull out a massive entrenchment below walls of Vicksburg's might. A tunneling tactic akin to termites, soil trashes topside to penetrate the enemy divide. Like digging under the skin soldiers burrow like maddening mites. Part of the 23rd flings earth, fixed wide-west, a flume from the left corner outside, bayonets brash and shine all to the ready, obliquely aligned. Invincible on sight, the infantry leeches tenacity in lunette stockades as sharpshooters line the ledge along a gorge, partners in war's crime. Dark redoubt-shafts arrange as so many anthills with odd awnings hanging on poles, which punch out of the hillside in precarious assorts and hide the soldiered mountain lions crouching and organized, ready to pounce upon prey in ferocious, horde-some fights. Jutting out of the rolling hills abatises bare tines. The sharpened dragon's teeth prepare to attack with two tons of black, gun-powder growling in immense seven by eight foot bites. Before Grant can tweak his strategy, true to his determined outline, multitudes are victimized in a sadly, Vicksburg cave life. Through Pemberton's stubborn will and pride the prized city's residents are trapped inside, coelesced with no where to hide. Thousands more deride a bloodbath outside the town's walls, subsequently besieged by Sesech fever and so stymied to the Union's cause; they litter the ground in mounds and die.

Those redans crop out at salient angles contoured to cover the Union soldiers hurtling hand-grenades and shells over their shoulders. Blue-lit fuses fly forward as it grows dark and a few come back and forth, which raises a relentless smoking storm. Our volunteers invade with inviable cloth, cut clean from visceral dedication and decorated with rapacious effort. Valiant through their spell of chores, vibrant landscapes play a pivotal ploy to Rebs vanishing into woods, covert deserters. The backdrop naturally sent astir from the rails to Mississippi's western shore. Inhabiting a self-made prison with Confederate munitions' hoards, the entire town aggrieves to starve with no one coming to reinforce.

Surging waves of brave Union defenders amass a nest aswarm, swoop in, and stinging. Opposing diametrically and obstinate as mules with dug-in feet, Rebs continue lambasting for years in diverse and stubborn pockets of Mississippi to resist the government plea, but these folks are nothing more than bushwackers, ostensible unto themselves and costumed as southern insurrectionaries. Whither the stout-hearted soldiers march north to south, west to east, they are indomitable as a team. Aptly energetic and unflappable willpower is forged of the highest degree. They push past heavy timber, up hard and dark, winding ravines. Chopping on, they trudge through high, acutely angled cane, thrash amid the underbrush, and tangle with Confederate troops, whom terrorize exceedingly. The Union march and fight unremitting, till they reach the northeast. Forces now surround Rebel redants by land with Sherman's north edged ruse, including the burgeoning, naval battle by the river west of the city. Vicksburg is thrashed and pommeled submissive. Confederates emasculate pathos and spit hatred and defeat, before deciding to concede and ultimately allow Grant to pocket his key.

Angry sons of the south sit sequestered inside; exigencies perilous, bequeath in defeat and mourning. In his customary gallant politics of war, General Grant allows them to surrender and more. Strenuously reluctant they do thus and spew severely tested secesh scorn. A Union control turns the tide on Mississippi's respectful "Munitions Lord". Ultimately rails, telegraph and supplies are seized and occupied to regenerate stores.

Pemberton sits poorly quartered in disgust on a battered porch among the disastrous debacle the war has rung of his fort. Grant arranges terms with an eye toward victory, but with respect inimitable for his foe, though he doesn't receive it likewise...Pemberton chooses to ignore. Nonetheless, an armistice proposal capitulates upon the garrison's force. White flags display along the lines as the Rebels outward pour. They sadly stack weapons; tuck rag-tag tails below. From once rugged troops a piteous transformation of pride occurs, when reduced to allowable, portable stores.

Humbled rebel officers, finally to horse with the rest of the lines, tread ejecting bitterness throughout Vicksburg's fort. Gracious Grant allows thirty odd wagons to assist them on parole heading north. (Months later Sherman gives orders for final assault to destroy and torch any supplies left they are unable to transport.) Befit America's glory to July 4; Grant gallops in leading Indiana's embattled 23rd volunteers, which follow Illinois' 45th in joyous report. A rousing rendition of "Rally Round the Flag" further bounces in echo as thousands sing with an earth-shattering roar, but their victory "party" is unexpectedly stopped short.

Grant in genteel respect for those he considers countrymen and comrades, albeit tragic, fallen unfriendlies, fellow soldiers and more, demands a somber approach, immediate on order. Waiting within the boundaries at Vicksburg on the other hand is disparaging malcontent, all manner of illness air born, starvation's last resort and frightening, fatality's gore. In the pocked streets, contraband tosses wildly in happiness like gracious, roses strewn for an imaginary king's honor. These gestures and gyrations though, add chaos more akin to thorns. Minding proper melancholy, Union business styles the first order. Already sapped, soldiers slap reins to a horse for the fort's initial take over and reorganization, solemnity of occasion to the fore.

The lowland swales tear the vile, wretch of refuge and the carpet of effluvium laid countywide, through vast channels of connective waterways, when at its worst. Moreover, thousands keep clamoring in the unclean environment for weeks, drainage poor. Dr. Birchett of the Vicksburg City Hospital cannot contain an endemic, rapid progression of the smallpox outbreaks holding court. After cooped up in cave lodgings, not to be ignored, town's people and their slaves raise the viral stakes to epidemic proportions. They scatter abhorrence, which requires a "Pest House outside the fort. To avert further contamination they burn bedding, fumigate and, when possible, quarantine incurables to prepare for remorse. Irony of need sees the very house giving safety to the regiment days before now signing death warrants from a foreign source.

A disease strangling folks with dreadful invisible fingers, territorial, the coward preys upon weak and those

young, old and infirm at health's core. It cowers pusillanimous with puss-filled sores. Infectious persons spiral into
fever, aching, scarred and forlorn. Convalescence is only
for the few, no longer at death's door.

Weeks of battle underscore and burden the populace
with a new catastrophe of war. Disturbing currents shift
in the rivers. From the months before hasty graves saw
shallow interment, but no more. Bodies in part and in
whole uncover a vile disruption for Vicksburg to endure.
Volunteers, martyred and war-torn, implore a manda-
tory, arduous effort. Hundreds already deceased are
dumped into ditches without respect to coffins or a service, just a little dirt hurled o'er. That is the one of the
anguishing consequences of battle's calamity across the
board. Realistic results of society's masses do lack hygi-
enic knowledge or soap and water support. The carnage
evinces military rancor.

With gratitude, though decades later, specifics of
wounding plight and heroism countrywide are shared for
years during gatherings of veterans at various and sundry
sites. Immediate account recognizes a man chosen to lead
for his might by his own men, ever eloquent, Lieutenant
Colonel Davis, moving valorous and righteous up the
ranks with his brother at his side in fight by victorious
fight. Steeling command of the 23rd volunteers like a sharp
Bowie Knife brandished from a Corinth Confederate
Davis as a trophy from the site. Entire respect from the
regiment for him and his brother is granted like the
Bible's "Sons of Thunder" railing side by side.

Leading the biggest little battle at Raymond accom-
plishes another victory, when they shift right as one

unit, two and a half hours against incessant affray to spite. Regiments of Indiana do not subside, blessed as well with assistance from Illinois undented, until mastery obtains over a hard won line. A deluge drenches and pelts our defenders, but they dare not yield their patriotic light. Indiana and Illinois troops from Vicksburg divide. General Sherman sends them in tandem toward Jackson, formation tight. Battle weary, soaked to the skin, but vigorously fit to fight. Strenuous as a notion of soldiery to sally, if ever seen so stalwart defined.

Lest we forget or be too ailing and declined in age to give half a mind, hundreds upon hundreds left unable to fight and those attending in hospitals gave their all in the thick of the firing line. Military machinations cannot complete objectives, unless a myriad of others give their all as well, behind the scenes of the gory grind. Duly noted are tireless surgeons, stewards, chaplains, volunteers and others who assisted selflessly throughout that troubling time.

Auntie Lucy, too, who worked as nurse, cook, laundress and mother, all duties required day into night. With her daughter as her shadow, amidst communal shows of tumult, they attend the sick and wounded, while death and disease were on the rise. The unfortunate consequence of these circumstances caused a careless and ignorant illness to best the old, infirm, and the littlest child. Merry Mona sadly came to her time working with her mom in the unhygienic clime. Lethal and viral smallpox transfers infection to the waning masses from an indefinite amount of forbidding fomites. There is no "win-win" in war's despairing design.

BITTERS WITH
THE SWEET

"Twas well through spring, '63, I 'membuhs bein' ovuh in Tenn'see an' full agin t'de top, blessin infuse'. Enlisteds sho do enjaw der time not allus on d'move. Dis be jus' priuh t'heading tow'rd Vicksbuhrg t'jine up wif othuh Union blues. We pull't up ahr boot straps fo' d'nex' battuh an' tryin' t'wuhrk up t'enthuse'. D'Fed'rals ain't got no man judgin' in d'midduh, hihr't t'heah sides fo' D'Great Dispute. No town meetin' on yuhr p'int o'view neithuh, t'have groups vote 'n' count up d'majawr'ty rule. It take puhrt neah a brick solid soul, doncha know, t'choose an' defen' abs'lute truth?"

"Often times, d'wifely folk wonts t'stay wif der men, mos'ly offisuhs en route. Unless d'men refuse, dese women come 'round from time t'time as pahrt o'de hospituh vol'nteah crew, gen'rally doin' d'sawrta thin' dat women folk do. Dey hep dole out d'pahrcels o'food an' read 'n' write lettuhs fo' d'men, when dey's in d'recov'rin' room. Wuhrst scenariuh t'imbue an' wraith shaduhs loom, presen'in' like bony finguhs o'clouds 'cross d'face o'de moon, jus' b'fo' a tuhrribuh, stawrm bring' on d'gloom."

"Mo' impawrt'ntly, dey prays wif 'em, when dat o'need too. We's in God's good grace 'round frien'lies 'n' neigbuhrly folk, den dose women hazard dawr-t-dawr huntin' donations o'linens 'n' food. Dey's hangin' 'round q'awrtuhs 'n' camps t'boot. Othuhs be cookin' 'n' laund'rin' a bit like me fo' a dime o'two. Cawrse, I jus' keeps muh head down, care fo' muh chile an' do muh chawrs 'n' duties."

"Scawres o'folks come t'visit an' see off der kin... knowin' it may be der last. Othuhs stop by t'drap off bread 'n' jams in baskets an' fresh shuhrts awll wrapped. Cawrse, dey's a passel o'men doin' what fam'ly do t'relax, huntin', fishin', picnickin' wif blankets on a patch o'grass, soakin' in d'but'ry sun an' bouncin' babes on der laps. Fam'lies in wahrtime is like washin' on d'line hangin' awll mismatch'. You jus' as likely flappin' in d'wind wif nuffin t'protect yuh an' op'n t'bein' snatched. Cawrse, yuh nahways safe wif Homegawrds makin' folks beg d'fense like a pawltry knee patch on yuhr las' pair o'rag'dy pants o'foldin' yuhsef, rejmental like, inta d'camps. I say, jus' as well take yuh chances in d'bivouacs. Dat was d'way o'thin's in d'days o'lawless attacks, keep yuhr enemy on yuhr front o'yuh's soon t'find 'em suhprizin' yuh wif a tap on yuhr back." Lucy and I jut our jaws into a nod and raised our brows of silent knowing that, the veteran art of sussing out a rat.

"In Memphis 'long 'bout uhrly May, befo' we's t'move soufwuhrd due, afta d'soljahs ends d'ev'nin's dress review, lotta bugaboo women, sneakin' 'n' loit'rin' t'intrude. Some 'dem gals be ole, some in der yout'. Dey sich'ate neah cities, wooin' lonesome soljahs fo' pay an' playin' 'em fo' foo's. I be eyein' pas' dem othuh group o'gals wuhrkin' t'uhrn keep in ill repute wif rej'ments neah dere 'n'uhthuh places like Nachez an' on d'Bayous. Cawrse, ev'ry town got d'unseemly gal o'two hangin' 'round fo' a bit mo' hullabalo. I seed 'em carryin' on mawr'ly loose, showin' der whatnots by d'saloons. Dey jus' en's up makin' ahr men sadduhle sawre, too tahred t'fight 'n' full o'booze, drinkin' till deys in a sickly stupuh. A sad tuhrn o' hawrse mah-nuhr 'n' hoopla fo' a straight shootuh."

"On occasion dem untamed gals' propri'ties gits a procliv'ty tow'rds d'uncout'. Dat' be when d'pi'us, white women on de ship might take 'em t'chuhrch wif a wuhrd o'two. De head o'de nuhrses in de hospituh, bein' ladies an' awll, bites a stuhrn pi'nt o'view off'n der b'hinds 'n' kicks 'em in d'provuhbiuh caboose. I see'd 'em do it! Ev'ry town 'n' camp's gotta few as a mattuh o'cawrse, but not bivou-acs o'de 23rd blues, Genruh Sanduhson dinna stan' fo' dat kinda bad news. Yuh see, d'ahrmy ain't takin' no sass fo' proof from any man, woman o'chile goin' nawrth o'souf o'de middlin' states wifout showin' athaw'ties d'propuh pass t'move on t'rough."

"D'mil'tary knows us gots a suhr'us wuhrk heah t'do. A doubuh pawrtion o'platoons o'men keep me an' ole Doctuh Bruckuh busy cleah t'nex' June. Sojahs an' city folk alike caught in d'cross hairs o'dis heah feud. Duhrin' d'battuhs we sawrts out d'woun'ed wif a quick look-ieloo. D'minuh ones gits patched an' sent on back, but d'mo' calam'tous cases git transpawrt Nawrth on d'ships t'de big hospituh at St. Lou'. Dat Missus Dix took reins wif d'wimin folk up dere t'git hospituhs full from d'top t'de root."

"Cawrse, some on d'mend, but der be mo' 'n' mo' kep' acomin' on in. Hun'erds, upon hun'erds comin' 'n' goin' on d'ships to d'hospituh by d'Rivuh, on d'wagons tryin' t'git t'de hospituh on Beale Street, to d'schoo' an' in dat hawse bein' used fo' d'Union headq'awrtuhs 'n' lodgin'. I heps dose folks in dat dwellin'—when d'smawllpox creep up like a backslidin' sin. Lawd knows dat dere a beastly ep'demic. Dey sends me up d'ridge t'count d'dead 'n' stip'late d'Pes' Hawse sick."

"B'fo' we gits t'headin' soufwuhrd boun', awll d'boys o'Indianny be strong like bull cows, healthy 'n' soun'. We be ready t'send dem Rebuhs back in t'dem caves in d'groun'. Not mo' dan a month in, we's stahrtin' t'go down, unfit fo' a head count. Men be wadin' in d'stagnan' swamp watuh waist high t'git t'fuhrmuh lan' inboun'. Dey's fightin' 'n' wuhrkin' fo' ahrs on en' wif d'insolen' sun o'summuh beatin' intoluhbuh profoun'. Fierce as d'iron wuhrkuh's fawrge come apoun'in' down, tuhrn't d'health o'de rej'ment entahr from solid t'hun'erds ailin' by d'en' o'wintuh wif ev'ry mis'ry t'e foun'. D'23rd plowed on down d'bivouac field by d'nawrtheas' an' stahrts whackin' tent stakes inta d'groun'. Thank d'Lawd fo' Ill'nois' 45th dat gots ahr back on solid groun'. Dem boys sends dose mutineerin' g'rillas tow'rd Jackson t'retreat, 'til supplies git comin' roun'.'"

"We wahrn't awllus within seein' distance o'rej'ments from uthuh states, but yuh heahrs d'shell an' shot comin' an' goin' jus' d'same. Dis heahr be d'singuh, lahrges' ahrmy o'folks I evuh see'd in one campaign. In Memphis d'hospituhs hol' pert neahr fo' hun'erd men apiece in a cupluh places, but as June lagged on wif fightin' 'n' diggin', we gots dat many comin' in sick 'n' dyin' o'dead ev'rday. Dat be a hahrd knock t'wake to an' not know who t'blame o'how t'keep yuhr wits on ev'n plane', but we gits through dat okay. Somehow we maintain ahr faith."

She wakes from sleep, not yet dreamt or rested, fitful and bent. A summer's shower strums on the tents unreasonable like nervous nails athwart a merchant counter disposed in frustrating pecks. Collected across canvas rooftops, spatterings ran in rivulets soaking down the hems. Rains reckon Lucy wake in the cheerless dark, check seepage to chills, and attend war's sullen, ill or wounded men. A small sacrifice to make without regret to ensure her daughter is not sold as a slave away from her; before rising she embraces Mona close to her breast.

Finding food is not as cumbersome this year as last year's quest, because families evacuated homesteads, dispossessed to the relative safety inside their Rebels' walled fortress. In retreat they leave a portion of stores, crops, wild berries on the vine, ripened and fresh, and fattened cows bellowing with milk and starving to death. Union troops take only what they need it is said. The food will rot and the cattle die, if not eaten. There's a bountiful amount of berries, nuts and herbs from the woods also to collect. Uncomplaining as usual Aunt Lucy embraces tougher challenges. She's no longer an ingénue and relishes gathering blackberries, lavender and sage with Mona, foraging freely on the woodsy edge. Tasks in the forest help to bring them back to their emotional, mental and spiritual best before heading to the hospital tents.

Parallel rows accommodated hundreds, filling beds. A slightly inefficient arrangement, albeit semi-permanent, proved in one sense an impediment when transferring quickly from one tent to the next. Shaded over by another tent is an oblong, centralized table for meetings or dinner on benches. It also holds multiple medical books, a mortar and pestle to mix concoctions from the dozen or more stoppered glass bottles of tinctures and powders, labeled and stored neatly in a large, wooden medicine chest. This isn't in use often to my recollection, but it's there, when surgeons are put to the test.

Lucy aids and abets Indiana's 23rd, Providence led, as if by extension caring for her own family crest, very dedicated. They offered to protect her family in what she understands as the Christian's quest. The full moon shines quixotic in that second year of service. By June many are unfit for duty's pledge. Injuries from firing and exploding shells, plus incalculable conditions for encountering ails exists is blamed on the waterway projects. All are kept from proving their best. Cooler, fitful nights, and manual labor, not to mention all day dripping sweat, sees the quantity of invalids and convalescence spread. Cotton bales, haphazardly dispensed on the ground near folks on cots, are a last resort as they run out of beds. Hundreds wait and hope, but cannot expect to be seen, angling awry in an unfrenzied disarray to occupy every space left. At times the moans of men ailing and maimed bereft, languish increduless or whimper in moans of torment, tremendous is the terrible distress.

It's not because the surgeons' working are ineffective, just insufficient. I would not jest. In fact purplish gray tinged skin sags around the doctors' eye sockets and cheeks, which were once ruddy and plump, but now droop as a bloodhound's jowls hanging exhausted from a snuffing out sickness and beg a protracted rest. Transversely, doctors undergo different sufferings from the soldier, but tests to faith and trials nonetheless. In one gut wrenching surgery after another, they brandish bloody arms and legs, chucking them crosswise to amass as a heaping-limbed-mess. Unfortunate, but now the expected norm, proceeds after each morn's gangrenous festering-wounds' inspection. Dispense chloroform, next hack with blade merciless, grind, gnaw and abrade saw into flesh. Soon enough sew the extra flap of dangling skin over the gap like a bulbous, badly bungled sock puppet. Dutiful doctors proffer a service to their country and mankind, tireless, and selfless.

The conduct of the climate contributes to the queasy discomfort felt by all personnel. Furthermore despairing, wounds put patients in varying states of duress. War's din, muzzle-loads muskets and groaning men, echo randomly visceral, whether northern or southern bred. By the end of June countless, Confederate deserters, some surprisingly dehydrated from dysentery and other considerable ails, surrender in the mix and lay quietly begging to be fed or simply to be left for a quiet end. These are those that want Pemberton to call a ceasefire and quell the blood shed, but the general's loyalty to Jackson and his skewed ardent attitude keep him steadfast instead. Controlled chaos begins to churn in Vicksburg like a gigantic kettle of fish head stew, stirred up and dished out, until all is fed and addressed. Mad misperceptions and rerouted routines meld "hurry-up 'n' wait" together in successions of food to cook and distribute, plus wounds to wash and dress and laundry to scrub and press. Lucy does her best.

Funerals as well, occur daily, inside and outside the city with a swaddle of sackcloth, if they are lucky. Partially disinterred and badly decomposed bodies are buried ill-fated, on a now broken and washed out levee. Crude wooden tablets mercifully carved with names and dates float freely, marking the end of each soul's journey hundreds of miles down stream. Inscrutable acts to witness, no vindication to be seen, for the Union's siege. Although both sides are incorrigibly crippled, they are no longer green and know there is no resting on laurels won or what seems to be a magnanimous victory. North and South will, it seems, maintain contrasting beliefs and subsequently, that is not a sign of the Union's battle relief.

"Inside d'fawrt d'23rd gits posts o'honuh high, select wif a few othuhs unnuhr Gen'ruh Blair puhrsuin' dem bullyraggin' g'rillas fo' a time. Octobuh's col' take us wint'rin' in Hebr'n, neah Vicksbuhrg, but jus' outside. What's left o'de reg'men' entahr sign' up fo' t'ree mawr yeahs o'dis grind. S'pose dat gonna git us t'de en' o'de wawr's line.

Dey's on d'Lou'sianny side 'long tow'rd '64, when Gen'ruh Shuhrman jine up wif us an' finish tannin' d'railroads' hide. Marching on from Jackson t'Muhrid'n, we be buhrnin' Confed'rate camps an' d'like wif a rivuh o'combatants, 500 cattle, an' dat many mo' contr'ban', so's d'Souf cain't use der supplies. Lawd have muhrcy on muh soul o'strife, dat be a lil talk fo' a lotta life. Reckon I gots go inta 'memb'rin' de wuhrs' time b'twix' Vicksbuhrg an' de rewahrds dat come due nigh, leastwise I's gotta try."

INVISIBLE TO SURVEY

"Vicksbuhg encountuh what seem like a sea o'dead. D'Good Lawd know' dat, when He see us bailin' blood by d'bucket. Sho nuff, keep us shawrt on recruits 'n' steam, while autumn's leaves tuhrnt gold'n. Dat jus' pahrt o'de reas'nin' we ain't moved encampmen' back t'Tenn'see come dese seven o'eight moon's chagrin' t'crescen'. Bless his hahrt, Doc' Bruckuh took ill an' scoot on back t'Indianny by then he jus' plumb wahr-spen'. Daily I be shuttlin', yonduh from tents in d'glen t'dat "White Hawse" on d'crest. Doc' Pheetuhs put me t'de test. I'se wat'rin' dose folks of de smawllpox threat an' countin' d'piles o'dead."

"Duhrin' dat time 'Renzo an' Chahrlie hahrbuh two beds on d'en'. Dey git shot up, dint o'shell in a g'rilla threat. Throwin' prayuhs cleahr t'Prov'dence, thin's bein' touch 'n' go, while dey's beggin' t'co'valesce. Po' lil Mo' ain't but fo' o'five yeah ol' an' cain't keep up d'trek, so's one day she say, 'Mama, t'day, I's gotta take a res'.' I give huh a lil peck an' fol' huh in on d'flo' side dose two God-feahrin' men an' says t'dem, 'Boys, I gonna tuck Mo' in heah fo ' a spell.' I shoot straight up d'hill, a Minnie ball spent. Honoh system an' merit t'check on dose folk an' git back t'de tent lick'ty-split, time fo' Mo' bein' rent an' awll."

The quashing, midnight rain tacks a freshness o'er the golden layers of fallen maple leaves blown aft. Beyond, emerald swales, wet and matted, roll into densely populated woodlands. The carpeted, earthy floor smacks of brackishness blended with rancid odors unfettered from war's masses. Fetid air overrides the ending storm's calming waft. Audibly alone on the redans, Lucy's issued boots tramp a smacking sound upon the moistened grime of prior clashes. The echoes of dormant squaddies' souls buried in combat are sleeping fast. Tracking up and around to squish in outlined stamps, the map of deep holes soldiers' spades and hired workers channeled to navigate, like a great many gophers or moles may craft, the choppy maze that had become the redans.

Since Lucy has been slogging up to the white "Pest House" from Logan's field-hospital, down yonder the moody bluff of hills undulating to the dell bearing off toward Jackson, four to five months have held fast. On the ridge of the final rise her put-upon-thighs give up a grunting exhalation, the pain from punishing muscle tissue does wrack. Four metal canteens strap on crosswise like banners upon her back, clanging in smacks against each other, her sides and her back. Weighty and cumbersome with water, four are all she can hack, plus lint and the bandage wraps, up the prominence she heads with that load as well in her haversack.

"Soon afta Vicksbuhrg give up der fawrt wifout much t'say, we be wuhrkin' up t'de "Pest House" jus' above dose redans t'care fo' d'folks dat's in d'wickedest, mis'ried way. Cawrse, d'stew'rds stocks us wif linens 'n' sich, but so many folks dyin' from wounds 'n' smawllpox ev'ryday, on accoun' o'pes'lence from d'unclean watuh an' folks pile't up in shalluh graves. Inside d'city, dey buhrns d'linens an' fum'gates dem kinda places. We spoons out soup 'n' med'cine an' sings 'n' prays an' tries ahr hahrdes' t'ease der las' days, but t'lil avail."

Upon the fuliginous fabric, a swath is cut of velvety black. Lucy is awestruck in a wondrous, visceral peace as she tilts her head to look up to the echelons and back. An eerie ring relishes luminescence around the moon's waxing expanse. Across a clearer atmosphere stars toss a warmer twinkling blanket of sundry-sized diamonds above, just-so tacked. The breather is basic to examine the sky and readjust her little physique straining under the sway of four disobedient watering tanks. Craning her neck as a graceful swan to track the pristine prismatic with canteens is tough to tackle, the maneuver throws her off balance. Mishap unto a declivity's scary incline almost pulls her back.

Recovering with a simple toe stubbing stumble and smile to the folly of her caliginous clanging, clunking sight, she says to herself, "Thank yuh Lawd fo' creatin' purty stahrs o'light an' keepin' me, Mo' an' d'folks dat's left unhahrmed an' upright. Maybe awll dem stahrs be standin' fo' d'anjuhs lightin' a canduh wif a spunk match fo' each o'de Christian sojahs dat die. Der dey go givin' us a wink now t'say, 'Doncha fret. We's home now, etuhrn'ly safe in Heaven. Trus' we gonna be aw'ight'."

Standing despite repeated shelling from afar, foyer columns show veining signs and battle scars. The generous oaken door creaks on its hinges, when she cracks it ajar. Her right thumb and forefinger pinch atop her nose and mouth in a sudden slapping alarm as an unspeakable, putrid odor quickly disarms. Lucy knows this means there are dead among the living and she must inquire toward finding out which ones they are, hence the surgeon pronounces them thus and covers them with a final, shrouding tarp.

Dutifully apt with compassion and a nurse's knack, Lucy trickles river water into arid, blistered mouths aslack. Gaunt, dubious faces warp and distort on bodies destructed with festering abscesses across arms and beleaguered backs. A swift-tic count of the passed and she's off, sprinting off like a jackrabbit tracked. On tiptoes she steps around them, not to ignore, but in respect, empathy and fear of stopping or staying to dilly-dally. Somewhat unable to breathe deeply, she doesn't realize she is holding her breath with a clamped hand, until she backs against a column outside and lets out a heaving, noisy flange.

Although he's delivering letters in Indiana up north, for some reason voices pop into her head of the Pastor. Lucy craves his charismatic sermons and encouraging words. They make her heart soar with passion for the Lord. Clement glimmers of more lanterns illumine the hills and dales in the diffuse darkness below as tiny spectral torches. Since newly wedding her husband, General Grisham's wife too, must be up early this morn. She has been on tour of the hospitals checking beds across the board. She beholds the thin tracings of lantern glow perched upon her bird's eye floor.

Reflecting alone this morn poured a fresh rosiness upon the apples of her cheeks from a time years before. Her life was held captive in repose, but she would peek out the kitchen window in accord, overflowing with joy and peace, simply watching Cal do his chores. She has not seen him, since they first left Bolivar more than a year before. Lucy can't wait till the war is over, so they can meet in freedom's glory and show Mona some distant shore. After pausing on the precipice to ponder a grander plan, she wants to fly as fast as she can to camp. A glad return to daughter and duties waits in the grassy glade of the upland.

"Offisuh Davis an' Gen'ral Grisham of newly connubiuh bliss come wif der wives an' gets settuh'd in d'lowuh levuh rooms o'de nices' hawse in Natchez t'regroup recruits. We'se gainin' stren'th fo' d'nex' campaign t'ensue. It take' long 'bout six o'sev'n month' t'git d'sizabuh 'mount o'troops, meanwhile we jus' keep' doin' what we's t'do."

Lucy immediately administers to Lorenzo Emery and Charlie Villiard, the first patients to be checked. Mona is still snuggled on a cotton bale in the corner on the ground by their cots in the central shelter. The two young men return from the trenches riddled with dysentery, a dehydrated mess. She hasn't set down her canteens yet, and as daily duty demands, she gives them sips of water, which are left. Unknown to her and them, the deadly smallpox virus transfers contaminants like the devil, invisible pollutants poisoning water seepage for all who partake from this sorry shaft of a well.

Ordered obligations to exact before she returns, Aunt Lucy tells the boys she'll be back to settle the round of clean bandages and light breakfast starters. She cradles Mona first, to nap in their private, casual quarters. Boiled black coffee, diced dried fruit and sliced fried pork, plus on peculiar junctures there are eggs, cream and butter for the officers' feast, which she must prepare, cook and serve.

Additionally, for a dime and sometimes more, she scrubs and plunges soldiers' cotton shirts to soak before hanging them to dry on a tether. Before the clock strikes nine she is back at the bedside of Charlie Villier and Lorenzo Emory, redressing the injured. As she is washing wounds and rolling bandages to cover them, Lucy's emotions sink nether and a shudder surfaces a tad upon discovering small pox blisters on their extremities, their heads burning with fever.

"Dem boys knew dey was gonna be ditched at de Pest Hawse on high by Doctuh McPheetuhrs. 'Auntie Lu', doncha fo'git us up der,' dey whispuhrs. 'If'n we take d'rag off'n dat las' battle, we's sure t'endure. D'Good Lawd know we ain't no bell ringers.' Dey's 'bout t'break muh hahrt fo' sure. I be pullin' out muh promises 'n' prayuhs t'see dem boys ev'ry sun's tuhrn. I's goin' t'de woods t'day t'fetch sumpin' fo' dat fevuhr'd mis'ry cure."

"No suh, mahrk muh wuhrd, der's no way t'do dis wuhrk wif out yuhr hahrt 'n' soul takin' a hawrse in full gallop, snawrtin' on his face t'de en' o'de race. B'fo' I be off, I gonna check muh sweet, tuckuhr'd young'un o'grace. When I rolled huhr t'me fo' a kiss 'n' embrace, she's in d'grips o'fevuh huhrsef wif fest'rin' sohrs all ovuh de place. Muh hawrse-sense is tellin' me t'take a knee an' git busy prayin'... fo' days 'n' days."

"Snared in a big, ole wagonwheel web I' be scare't peaked 'n' pale like d'fly dat gots awll wrapt 'n' dazed fo' a spiduh's taste. '*Lawd, tell me what t'do!*' I close muh eyes t'plead 'n' beg. Sho nuff I heahs in muh head, 'Sage.' I snaps muh finguhs, grabs a pig stickuh blade an' heads t'de wooded way. I'muh walkin' an' wishin' Pastuh Roguhs be comin' back t'day, 'cause feahr's grippin' me t'strang' late. I swear it gonna ovuhrtake muh faith. 'Mama's gonna fix it muh lil babe. Right now, I be off t'de wood an' find some sage. Yuh jus' lay heah an' res' muh anjuh. We's gonna git yuh fit as a fidduh. It gonna be okay.'

"I spins roun' left 'n' right, plum frantic as a whippet chasin' a 'coon. Ovuh d'swales I be rushin' 'n' prayin' d'Lawd t'lead me as I heads down t'wahrd d'wood. Sudden-like, as d'Awlmighty Lawd would, atop d'track ridge hitchin' a ride from d'west in d'grav'ly, dry sawl unduh foot, I espy some spin'ly, wild sage done took root. 'Bout knee high d'long-tongue, bumblin' bees gits set abuzz real good."

Lucy bends down to whiff a slightly peppery odor exuding true, though the paler cornflower color as well is a clue. On the throat of the spikey whorls it expands like a pitcher making landing pads perfect for an insect brood. The powdery spreadwing skipper reaches the bull's eye first, nestling nectar's syrupy good. Visitors zoom in centrally from the neighboring wood. A coosome two-some of brush-footed butterflies flit to the party fashionably overdue, thus they wait for room to dip and swiftly sup from the foliage's skyblue hood.

Tough, floppy rugose flail at the wind's command upon wiry shoots, long leaves of grayish-greenery with soft-haired underbellies unfolding to meet suitors of late October blooms. She digs around a plinth of wooden rail, clawing into the dirt and pebbles with her calloused hands near the taproot. A solid double-yank upon the shoot musters with panting grunts of urgency to heave the plant forth as only a mother's saving soul can do. Grasping them with her left and dangling dirt and dragging root, she puts her other hand to her forehead upon standing to survey the view. Lucy looks frantically down the track for some more stems flagging greeting and waving her through. With the hurried step to meet them she gives a proper jerking to them too. Supplied sufficient with medicinal herb gathered to concoct a healing tea's brew, she tucks the plants, roots and all, into an apron crease and bolts back to check on Mona who is growing feverish with a chill like flu.

"Mama' gonna mix up some spe'shuh sage tea. Dat gonna fix yuh up muh lil bumbly bee, bright as a shiny, coppuh penny." Then she mumbles to herself. "I bes' rustle up anothuh batch fo' 'Renzo 'n' Charlie."

Lucy tosses an extra rubber covering atop Mona's tiny shoulders and swabs sweat from her brow that has formed like dew in little beads. Initiating a plucking and piling spree, she preens and pulverizes until all stems are simply naked of sage leaves. Above some smoldering embers, always at the ready, waiting to be set aboil for cooking or laundry and such as need be, a huge pot of water saves her additional time trekking back over to the nearest stream. She rubs a verdures handful and lets the primed essence flake off with a clap-clap into earthenware crockery. As the fire burns she adds a drop of whiskey and two pinches of sugar to sweeten. She stirs the tincture slowly with a weathered, wooden spoon to increase the rising, aromatic heat.

Though the camp's activity is in full swing, the movements around her are indistinct as if another breadth of time is between them and her. Lucy goes about her various tasks with a serious gait against her usual style and demeanor. Although pleasant as blue to an October sky when addressing her work, an uncalculated fear sneaks up to stagnate and fester. Interchange occurs with Dr. McPheeters about a wounded soldier and an officer gives clear discourse to clean his described shirt, but she can't tell you what words exchange as they converse. She just nods to them both to be sure. A throb in her heart pines to be by Mona and give her worth in their lesser canvas tent as a caring mother, not as a dutiful nurse. She chomps through her chores and does just that, turning gale-force front to attend to her daughter, practically flying right by one of the "Willie" stewards.

Colored ashen, the babe's amber skin bares worsening eruptions gone excruciating vile. Dim and darkly circled eyes have lost their customary, innocent merriment and twinkling smile. Positioned on the cot like a pen-thin line is just a child, Mona weighs in without an ounce of guile. Subsequent upon straining the tea, Mama Lu' lifts a feeble head flushed forlorn and slightly sweaty above the cotton pile. Unseen and inexorable an adversary grips gloomy within her child. God help her, if anyone finds out, Mona will be sent to the "Pest House"…exiled. Lucy tries to rein in concerns unrefined, but she keeps cultivating frenzied confusion about Providence's design.

She says to herself with indignation as if confronting a slave master, riled, *"Ain't nobody but God gonna take muh chile."* Then aloud, her voice wanes overly soft and calm, "Take a lil sip muh babe. Le's keep dis mis'ry a'bay fo' awhile."

Dipping a cotton cloth carefully into a container of water, she squeezes it out solicitously, swabbing gently, as only a mother be led. Then she poses it delicately on her daughter's forehead and begins prayer in silence, but ends aloud with "Amen". Mona sleeps like the dead. Lucy bends closer kissing her head, whispers her return and swears sugared affection, breathless to fight tears' best. Hurriedly she hangs her spare canteen crosswise on her shoulder before she leaves to the parapets. She insists on lugging homemade brew for her two favorite boys sent to the house on the crest. Wiping a wetness cresting in her eyes, she sucks up a heavy, sighing breath and gives Mona's palm a press. The sage beverage sits brewing in the sun outside the officers' mess for a bit, because she has to stew vittles for a spell, in due time it will be brought to Charlie and Lorenzo yet.

Soon the savory smell of pork 'n' field beans sizzles in the air and mingles with fresh, strong coffee. Lucy tops it off with dandy slices of dried peaches stewed in a bit of sugary brandy. The officers don't seem to notice she is present in body, but in spirit absentee, hungering not for food or even spirit, but for chores to be complete. Yearning as well, to keep her pledge of guarantee to Lorenzo and Charlie and take care of little Mona's needs. She secretly wishes wise Pastor Rogers' sojourn up to Indiana's New Albany brings him back with speed, so together they can take a knee. His way of extolling and entreating the Lord always strengthens beliefs.

"Lawd in Heav'n keep Pastuh Roguhs safe from hahrm and in his travuhs God speed." She prays too for Mona, another silent prayer of need. While the officers' go on with more coffee and meetings, Lucy cleans.

Finally, after completing her cooking and laundress roles, as well as nursing rounds expected back at the hospital gazebo. She trudges the terraced rises and reconvenes up the awkward ramping redans to come upon the house on the plateau with a precious canteen cargo of healing tea in hold. When she touches the top, dress review is underway down below, streaks and strict patterns of men parade on review for show. Aunt Lucy doesn't look up to the stars or back down below. Anxiety looms on approach. October closes evenings down a might cold, yet she sees the lads sitting outside with their backs against the stone. Just as bowled over to see her doling out specialties on patrol are Charlie and Lorenzo. They take thoughtful sips and bless Aunt Lucy for the trek on the whole. They tell her, if they are going to expire, they'd rather be taking their last in God's fresh flow, than sucking some sickly, sesech, townsfolk's blow.

Lucy nods without much ado or small talk to get on the go, "I's gonna try an' rustle up a coupluh rubbuh blankets fo' yuh to offput the col'. Be seein' yuh in d'mawrnin' though fo' sho'."

Back down the maze of redans she gallops, clomping with canteen aclang, to feed and check on Lil Mo'. Like the picket on patrol with upper lip bit stiffly, for three days she repeats this rigid routine. The morning of the third day the sores seem to fade away on Lorenzo and Charlie, a miracle unforeseen. Dawn yawns creasing another night's sheet, but Lucy does not appear on the pest house porch, per her routine commanding the habitual set of clanging canteens. This blustery, autumn sunrise has neither seen her on the field. The boys want to share their recovery.

It will have to be decreed they are free of disease by one of the doctors before they can be released. They trot to Dr. McPheeters and their clean bill of health is received. He rubs stubbly chin whiskers in curious concern and asks for a check-in next week. He quantifies without reprieve that they are in fact ready for duty. Lorenzo and Charlie know Providence's Hand has intervened or has given Aunt Lucy the wit for healing tea. After a quick meal of coffee and field beans they double-time it to distinguish Lucy in thankful express before heading on to a couple of pickets' grateful relief.

Glaring and abrupt, the familiar bugling blares out a clamorous, wakeup revele.

They rush to the slit opening and call out, "Mawrnin' Aunt Lucy. It's 'Renzo and Chahrlie. We are fit as fiddles and want to thank you kindly."

They look at each other popped taut with grins upon their cheeks. When there is no reply, they say it again with a rising tone of query and sneak a peek. She's wilted inside the tent as a dying leaf no longer green, kneeling flat on her heels atop the grievously unsympathetic, dead grasses of the field. Ever so softly, slowly humming Amazing Grace, she rocks her torso slowly forward and aft to a pacifying beat. Diminutive to the dark shadows inside the tent, Mona's lifelessness hung heavy. Mama Lucy refuses to move her arms, but they are growing weak.

Their declaration deems peculiarly sweet, so she turns to look from whence the sound proceeds. As she turns her neck directionally toward the triangular pleat a harsh ray of light spills stark witness like a puddling bleed, exposing the scene, tragic and ghastly. Pleasantries laid waste to view for the youthful men with a silent gasping shriek. Beneath the faded, canvas shroud Lucy lingers in an uncommon glowering panic, staring up at Charlie with vacant, saddened eyes, puffy, red and glistening, but does not speak. The agony of her mind is beyond comprehension and dust on tear trails stream in two tiny creeks. Since they have just come from the "Pest House", bodies bespattered in smallpox sores are a known reality, but still they stand in disbelief.

"Auntie Lu', wwwe're gonna get ppastor…uh, uh and, and the Doc'," they manage to splutter a sputtering utterance.

"It coulda been a finguh snap o'maybe hahrs 'til dey return'. I still 'membuhs d'blest Pastuh Roguhs han' on muh shoulduh gentuh an' fuhrm. 'Lucy, Mona is wif d'Lawd now, yuh can res' yuhr concern.' I look up t'him an' I 'membuhs a puhrfec' light shinin' b'hind 'im bluhrrin' his fechurs, but I jus' says, why? I prayed daily t'keep huh safe from hahrm… unhuhrt. Precious lil Mo' has died anyway, unabuhl t'scape fate's tuhrn."

"Pastuh Roguhs counsel' me sof'ly, 'Ahr Redeemuh, who know d'en' from d'beginin', decide' when ahr puhrpose' time come due. If'n it be huhr time, ain't nothin' yuh can do. What yuh choose t'do wif *yo'* time lef' t'serve, now dat up t'you. If'n yuh ain't sacrifice' awll wif a massa' in puhrsuit, Merry Mona may haf suffuh't d'same fate wifout evuh knowin' d'Lawd o'de joyous bon' 'tween yuh two.' He' d'mos' gospuh smahrt man I evuh knew."

She trusts the pastor implicitly, but presses her child to her chest like the fragile gift of a budding rose. He stretches his arms toward her to take the body rightly slow. Mollifying his tone to allow Aunt Lucy to relax her weary hold and completely exhausted… let go. He calmly tells her to wash up, wait there and let him and the boys make this a day to honor Mo', a day to rejoice that one of the Lord's children has returned home. Lucy does as she is told.

GREATER PLAN REVEALED

Unmanly welling submits anew and therein stays. How has Lucy graciously governed yesteryear's pain and gain? Eight and thirty autumns cast away still engender tears for her precious, lost babe. Subsequently, I sink teeth into my lower lip a second time to keep focus straight. My proper pen falls flaccid o'er the page, yet again dragging in disquiet across the paper, for what to say. This time I do not offer my hanky her way. I have begun to develop a keener perception of her métier, her pride and her life's pace, so I pat my eyes and put it away.

In brief hours Lucy's rendering tale disconcerted a heavy-hearted stone, amply unfastening from its place. Throughout the rage of our country's angriest age Mona may surely be the youngest innocent and nurse's helper of my knowing affected by the arena's embittering plague. Immeasurably altered, I'm unpredictably hit by a thunderbolt of change. Shovel-smacked to the brain and whacked wide awake from my fragmented faith's deep-sleep state. The colorblind death of her daughter's doomed and sobering fate witness love unchained. I no longer saw black or white, friend or foe, just a mother with a dying babe.

Images suddenly blaze over a montage of smokey acreage where deafening acts of tragedy staged in theaters of war outplay. My brothers in arms still, fully drenched in the grisly irrigation of flooding crimson stains, inglorious they lie in unmarked graves. Capes of coats cover their faces, burial shrouds to shelter where they lay. Should not the demise of every patriot fallen in our country's service be honored the same? Should not a blameless child martyred be worn abreast as a red letter baring society's shame?

God help my exception to these soldiers of life, stalwart and brave, I choose to fashion a calumnious void, unknowingly dazed. As if to join them irrationally constraining to their tomb, and thus a foolish culpability maintains. If I were to stay alive, purely perfunctory it would be to ever so slowly snuff my own life's flame. I reach and place a hand resolutely on Lucy's to find an answer for my own disbelief and my self-disdain.

"How do you continue with another campaign? How do you… survive the grief without blame? Where is she laid to rest?" I hear myself eventually effuse with a certain solemnity made. Met there with ancient eyes of effulgent wisdom, sparkling deep brown as wet-splashed, earthen clay Lucy reacts staid.

"Miss'sip still gots huhr boxed in a Vicksbuhrg grave. Fo' o'five yeahrs afta d'wahr 'twix' d'states I takes d'Natchez back down d'Miss'sip' way, so's Mo' git propuhr respect paid. Cawrse huh bit o'lan' ain't mahrked wif sticks o'stones t'say dat where she lay. None o'dem sawrry souls got done dat way, but Pastuh Roguhs still gif wuhrds o'peace 'n' grace."

All the "Willie" stewards gather piles of wild flowers as a group with Charlie and Lorenzo. Another bunch hammers a pint-sized, common board coffin to go, while others dig out the perfect sized pit in a peaceful spot by a shady meadow. Not forgetting anything to assist with the moment's hope, the musicians are informed of the need for a solemn hymn to suit Lil Mo'.

Burials and funerals have been inevitable, not an unusual occurrence, if time and circumstance give room for show, since landing in Mississippi over five month's ago. The melancholy muffle of the "Dead March" rattles the paradiddle to a rudimentary crescendo. Comrades commanded by the corporal march with arms low. The rough-hewn wood is covered with the stars and stripes, when an officer goes or, if possible, a flag is held, while a curling gust blows. The ambulance may fetch a body, soldiers lower the coffin into a grave and volleys are fired by the guard after others fill the hollow, not like loss by the warm hearths of home. Men long in service may squelch or disallow the maudlin waft of show, pervasively waste energy like warm air out an unclosed, winter window. Be it bivouac, on the go or a stationary field fortification, intimate, sentimental energy is more often penned on paper by a fireside glow, this day's demise is different though.

Chaplain offers assistance to Aunt Lucy by a touching, supportive limb's walk to a clearing by the trees. Then an ambulance wagon arrives with the coffin covered in creamy magnolias, blue lobelias, tiny petals of star-shaped red flowers, clusters of rusty-colored blossoms and buttery, dainty daisies. The boys in blue go beyond with a plethora of rainbow beauties for this soul of sweet innocence, Mama Lucy's shadowing sheen. Mona brought smiles in the past year and a half that beamed, brighter than the struggles and strife seen along the way by every rank throughout the company. It is bits of optimism like these which invigorate requisite hope in good deeds.

All the men have seen her grow with glee; regardless the reference term coined her as 'lil pickaninny'. Some would hoist her onto the supply wagon as a toddler to nap safely out of harm's way on the pile of coats, pelts or bags of fleece, when long marches weary a happy little helper serving hospital Union armies. The officer and adjutant made sure she had shoes and a new garment at last year's end.

Pastor Rogers, as custom, presents a most poignant expression of speech leaving no eyes dry or noses clean. "Lord we commend to you this day the sunniest spark our eyes have seen, Mona Higgs, who bears with us in service, throughout this awful warring time of our great country. She is not only one of your children Lord, who prays and believes, she is one of our patriotic supporters, diligent as exemplified by her mother's caring creed. Father in Heaven, we thank you also for leaning this burden our way, so we can comfort our Auntie, Lucy. If you had not sent her to us, many would not have wounds…or shirts cleaned. Many would not have known her tender care or good eats, when times are lean. Impress upon us Father to watch over her the same… in her time of need. Angels cradle Mona's spirit to ascension with speed."

A tall fiddler pulls his bow across the violin strings sweetly slow, humbling in melancholy art. Lucy quietly whimpers and then weeps hard from an inconsolable hurt marking this period of her life, notched scars on a broken heart. As a whole the experience joins the soldiers beyond arms, like welding shards to a sturdier steel frame from individual parts. As the pastor speaks some of the striking flora the men have gingerly spread atop the box wave in the late morn waft. Before the four men lower her into the long trench fragile petals flutter off and pull apart. Intimate ceremonies such as this, interwoven with sincere tenderness from the start, move the group to evolve and bond more like a family, since the birth of their journey in Bolivar.

"Listen please, past your grief. The disposition of God's greater plan reveals itself with each soul released, not for them, but for us. Don't you see?" Distinguishing words of the chaplain reverberate to redans in the rear of our gloomy gathering at Mona's meadowed hillside of peace. He pauses and searches a small sea of crest fallen faces across the company. "Every soldier that bleeds, including our most radiant loss yet, Mona… will be free. Hold no fears for love or idly sadness cleave, for dear ones, those lost live in eternity. Love demands our soul, our life, our all in all… It is this courage to love that lives in every essence of our being." Pastor Rogers looks up to the sky, which had grown grayish and bleak, but a sunny shaft shines through as if angels have split the billowy cloud banks to witness and listen to the stirring scene.

"Honor them by letting your love for Jesus, for humanity, for your country and *by God for each other* reign supreme. Know, if not for this child, Aunt Lucy would not have been here to serve us as laundress, cook and tender hearted nurse in our times of need. Take heed during our short time on this earth to encourage one another as did merry Mona's simple smile encourage every deed." The Chaplain's message, an inspirational bell, rings confidently clear and bonafide free, as it usually does for the men...and for me. The Lord's Prayer finishes his homily with a customary chorus of 'Amen' and another pleasing hymn, which ends quite worthy. Soon each walks off to normal wartime duties."

I feel wings of Grace fondly lift me from my self created chasm to forgiveness and accept God's plan for my fate. All other privations and hardships fall comparatively, faded away. In due course understanding submits my purpose plain...write Lucy's story, share her journey's pain. Presently alluding to my bond of empathy, I close my eyes and shake my head with condolence of that tragic day.

"Mo' dan a thousan' men taste der las' bref from nawth t'south o'gun-totin' blame. One on top d'othuh dey' laid... shamefuh too many t'sawrt in a hun'erd days. Thank d'Good Lawd fo' d'nobluh men o'de 23rd dat rally' t'keep me sane. Dey treat' Mo' as one o'der own an' walk' me through d'dahrkes' rain. Unknown t'me on dat day d'Lawd sent hep muh way. John Nichuhs lighten d'grav'ty as d'res' o'de men walk away. He mos'ly a stranguh t'me ev'n den, but as a man o'de coluh't race, sho nuff from time t'time I see'd his face.

"I be lef' t'muh own reflection at Mona's grave, gazin' down in a daze' dismay. A strange feelin' wash' ovuh me t'wont t'dig huh up an' I plunge' muh finguhs int' d'mawis' clay. Sudden-like by d'foot o'de grave d'sof'es' fid'lin' tune b'gin t'play an' muh mis'ried emotions arres' der state. Wif eyes close' I be lis'nin' t'de hymn's ac'lade from dat lone fig-guhr an' I stahrts t'hum 'n' sof'ly sing, "When I Survey…" When he finish doin' it justice, he put a han' t'muh head an' walk' away. I nevuh looks up his way. It wuhrn't till yeahrs latuhr I finds out Johnny be d'one 'hind d'Lawd's savin' music dat day. Awll dem deaths neahr Vicksbuhrg cas' a gaunt shadduh o'gloom ovuh d'whole comman', 'spesh'ly when Pastuh Roguhs gots t'add t'Colonel's repawrt 'bout muh lost bright, anguh's ray."

～,ᛁ～

You never know, unless you stay the course, when things are going to turn around for the better…or for the worse. A cursory mend of sorts is eventually sewn across the harrowing death of her small-pox spurned daughter. Though there is an urge to restore the raw, gaping seam in her heart, she braves almost thirty battles to the tally-ho's surge, no allowance made for a pleading, cathartic purge. Woebegone in war's worldly travesty to distraction, but still, an unquenchable flame of grief does smolder and burn.

How often do we not yearn for times much simpler? The tussling realization tugs, when a loved one's final separation occurs? Physically we may know and understand the matter that they are with God in that instant, a place gloriously better, but yet we seem to want them with us again, blast the cost or what ever. My illustrative case found time alone heals and faith perseveres. We then continue, fearless or not, in our journey through this wild, willful world. I know now I am here by His persistence, so I stare into the recesses of her eyes and wait patiently adjourned. Like a man who climbs the craggy cliff hoping to hear wisdom from some bearded, cross-legged hermit's antediluvial response to the meaning of life long unanswered.

CAMPAIGNS COMPLETE, CARRY ON

Major Hooper takes her into his home as housekeeper and cook at a minimal wage months later, when a 30 day furlough comes, welcoming as spring in March. Circumstances anticipate knitting new and novel yarns, albeit a time of war. Dr. Brucker's original promise of army pay for her nursing skills still grows as a hope in the seed he'd planted by her mind and heart, but overall, she has to accept the fork in her purposed path shorn of Mona and Cal's love and charm.

"Sawl'tary t'muh nightly cot at Majuh Hoopuh's kind regahrd, I's he'pless 'n' gracious in one swif' swahrm o'feelin', sawrta like a body wifout ahrms." She cocks her head sideways to the left, directionally looking out with a stark-brown eye like a curious cardinal. Lucy speaks rather slowly as if she ponders it to her own disarm. "Losin' a chile be mo' akin t'lost limbs dat once be a pahrt o'yuh whole dan like losin' sumpin' not attached as a gahrmen'." Empathy's possibility may be from care to heartrending veterans in a hospital ward. I take pause with a mental visual on guard.

"Auntie Lucy" is acknowledged respectfully on everyone's lips, a dignified and devoted individual who stays to do her part. Point in fact, the battle worn survivors consider each other with such high regard, all reenlist, returning in body as weathered soldiers on the next march. By their native artisan trade, steamboats, they travel up the Mississippi, Ohio and Tennessee Rivers to pass through four states in part. Substantial artillery assaults transpire on two mountains and while forging three creeks as the Rebels continue to spar.

That muggy Midwest summer of '64, officers quickly change their lead due to casualties' regard. General Gresham, who refuses to get puffed up newsy notices in his typical gravelly charm, is wounded in the knee near the Chattahoochee on July 15, before dark. For the rest of his life the unfortunate event makes him lame-hard. They send him packing, back to New Albany, Indiana on medical discharge.

Hardly a week later, on the first afternoon battle by Ezra Church yard, boldly brave and beloved General McPherson dies, when caught face to face with opposing forces off his guard. Plowing a gap between his sixth and seventh corps, Confederates surprise him from the flanks with bayonets blazing as he rallies at full gallop to deny the hazard. After stopping short upon seeing his enemy, he turns hard, but is shot and killed, thus General Logan infamously leads the charge. Grand Atlanta is finally seized from entrenchment, while enduring constant fire. The Army of the Tennessee refuses disregard.

The quickening end the North hopes for prolongs three years plus to date. Original terms reach expiration for initial officers and discharge papers are raised. Recruits and promotions from within do promptly replace vacancies, nevertheless by early September another swain leads the fray into pugnacious skirmishes, which sustain unabated. General Sherman beleaguered for battles to end and frustrated at the delay, arrogates groups in a combined carnage and forage operation upon the populace and landscape for his latest calculated campaign. Special field orders regulate rearrangement of his army southeastward and looping toward the north, while Grant keeps Virginia sequestered in a stalemate. Events chart stern obligation. They link a dramatic chain crosswise the nation to demand supplies in this new mission.

New Albany, Indiana is never burned or burgled by an infantry's charge during the years of the Civil War, but an unruly state of affairs carbuncles. From what you read it starts with deeply rooted religious beliefs on the one hand and the other offers heavyhanded politics at its heart. Laws for slavery over Ohio's River are quite different, of course. Like putting the horse behind the cart the differences throw additional hotheaded matters across bordering parts.

Scathing battles south never occur in Hoosier territory, exception taken to Morgan's Raid of 63'. Regardless of their Union call to arms, Indiana's population convulses, particularly conflicted voices mount the subject of slavery. Persistant factions decidedly charged and extreme in action are opposed diametrically. Granting allegiance to the gracious cause, Second Presbyterian Church influential leaders brazenly preach, unrelenting and openly about antislavery. Other leaders in the state like Governor Morton, claim an abolitionist lean, but seem to be stuck somewhere in the middle without much resistance or recourse, politics done fashionably. Indiana leaders debate consequences of egalitarian ethnicity both privately and publicly. Unprepared for rapid growth like unpruned, root bound ivy, the ex-slave exodus ensnarls cities insufferably. Still in custom, merciful charity sews and distributes shoes and garments near West Union, glory to bounteous generosity. The larger community of blacks in the city prioritizes a need before and after the Civil War from New Albany's gracious American Home Mission Society.

Certain pockets of prejudice, the *Indianapolis Journal* and *Daily Sentinel,* as well as New Albany's *Daily Ledger,* print to attest for bigots and racially discriminatory designs, which buttress their hatred of blacks in hostile articles, oppressive in overtones to further fuel upstarts. Potent as copperhead poison to the population, the printed word swells townsfolk to a mob mentality for years during the war. Even town meetings and debates cause superfluous party upheavals and catch many tiptoeing fences, teetering off guard. Contemptible, jarring race riots too, mar and scuttle groups of blacks out of town, right from their own backyard. Abominable, entitlement retaliations among unscrupulous figureheads of high position in Indiana's government as well, defy opponents in unthinkable and rebellious; self-suiting laws foisted against "freedmen" and circle them like sharks.

I suppose Lucy and the soldiers are more content in the "clan" of the 23rd where, even though times are hard, dutiful choices make sense, hard work, honor and the last vestiges of integrity gratefully replace hypocrisy's almagamation of emotional and political garbage. Civil War's antagonistic hostilities aren't over and neither are possibilities of death or harm.

➤╱┃╲◄

"Did you ever consider staying in New Albany farther away from a battlefield's sparring?" I asked what appeared sensible questioning to an interviewer's art, but Lucy has survived some of the world's peak points of insensitivity and uglier parts. Rhetoric's obvious response is apparent before her sentence starts, so I thank her for her warm invitation and refined accommodation thus far, as she clears our repast away with an easy clink of empty tea jars. A lengthening shade from the porch casts wider across the front yard.

"I knowed by d'Pres'dent's Proc'amation I be free at large, but I be boun' t'dem boys an' men in muh charge. Dey's not only one o'de bes' thin's dat's evuh hap'n t'me, dey's been muh only fam'ly, since d'wors' o'de war hit muh spuhrit hahrd. Dese be d'folks I trus' t'have muh back, when d'goin' gits hahrd. Cawrse, quick as dey pick up der arms, mos' dem so'juhs gits accustom' t'camp, d'routines an' outdo' chahrm. Soon, I sees a few asmokin' pipes, othuhs be playin' chess o'cahrds o'writin' lettuhs t'loved ones back home t'fahr away Indianny fahrms. Mo'ovuh, Pastuh Roguhs' witness 'n' mawruhl messages… on D'Good Book an' d'Lawd… dat be mo' precious dan a treashuhr ches' o'gol' t'gahrnuh."

As far as they are concerned, after surviving Mississippi battles, accompanying Sherman onward to the Meridian raid of 1864 is something of which to look forward. Affording adventure's verve without excessive alarm an embattled battalion heads straightaway to march. New commands, a stern necessity of war, destroy hundreds of miles of Secesh supplies and arms and keep additional supplies from reaching south, but it may have taken things a tad too far. There are railroad ties torn asunder, telegraph-lines ripped and tangled, barges and bridges burned to char and exploitable stock or property appropriated by force at large. Tecumseh, tantamount to destruction, is bent upon ruining or seizing anything of military value that might allow sesech ideas and armies to waltz through with war parties and continue filling their current dance card.

Although President Lincoln and General Grant have reservations, far fewer men are slaughtered by these strategic marks. Corralling nomadic herds of cattle and partnering to forage, parties form to feed this vast section of the Union's army. Furthermore after each battle, numerous freed slaves merge the lines, not as contraband or prisoners, but with no reward. As the emancipation is underway thousands enlist in colored troops and take up arms. Other freed slaves remain to embark on the extensive expedition as well, amassing suddenly and growing by the hundreds without warning. Far-reaching, the expansive spectacle of men and beasts belts a brash, wide margin.

From February of '64 to spring of '65 Lucy resumes prior chores: bring hot coffee and cool water to those panting with parched desire and keep another pot ready to boil on the fire, bandage the wounded or at least pull them out of the field of fire and give prayerful comfort to men in their dying hour, as well as wash occasional officer shirts with bluing starch. Primary army responsibilities are earmarked by savory delicacies fried in lard, which Lucy rustles up for officers with herbs foraged from forests and farms. Meantime in May, the Indiana's 23rd traveled by steamer, train, two boats and a big old barge. Quite a long trip to get to the battle at Bird's Point, hit on Huntsville hard, clamor Confederates in Cairo and bang up bridges on the Black River before they can head east to the Atlanta march. She remains in service north with them on to the Carolinas' charge. Another courageous campaign starts, but instead of parking her horse, Lucy charge remains faithful to God first and the Indiana's 23rd volunteer soldiers, until the end of the war.

Sherman's reticulated attack angles northerly to stay the circuitous course through the spring of '65 and Johnson's surrender. However, it is General Robert E. Lee's silver-haired, somber features capitulating rigidly in the McLean mansion's sitting room chambers that resound a louder departure for the great Dispute to render. His admission of defeat instantly creates thousands of Confederate prisoners. Respectfully equanimous as always, Grant gestures by a tip of his hat and is followed in suit on that note to salute by his officers. Sad as a southbound mouth the Rebel challenge is resolved, nearly a presidential term later, barely a click and a bit from the initial instigators.

Families rejoice at the northern conquest, but beg God to make America whole again. No sinecure comes to broken constitutional intent. Providence is not quick to recompense our country's sins as many an embittered soul on both sides refuses to repent. Assassinating the Great Emancipator exemplifies such, a week from the initial success. Extreme elation trumpets, folks flock the streets in triumphant express, but now, mourners flock to lament a President's passing, an irreprehensible tragic event. People from northern states, young and old alike are sorrowful and unsuppressed at the official processional and line streets in excess before "Honest Abe" is laid to rest. A mizzling mist of angel tears follows from the sky spattering in periodic protest toward Abraham Lincoln's death.

——

Lucy lumbers back from the quaint little kitchen all her own with a faint thwack, thwack. I hear her cane's placement, unmistakable as it lands. A familiar creak, I hear and then …"WHAP", the door's screen slamming. My long grin won't surpress, when slumped shoulders jump at the sound of wood on wood clacking. She shakes her head a touch with a teeth sucking, tsk-tsk and a little lip smack.

"Lawd, have muhrcy. Sawrry 'bout dat… Yuh know, I 'mem'buhs d'sad day o'de blest leaduh Lincoln's passin'. When d'Genruh git wuhrd of it, he awrduhrs awll in d'procession t'stop fo' a time o'silent respec' 'n' prayin' fo' d'muhrduhr o'dat great man. We's awll weepin' 'n' low fo' d'courage he had t'lead dis troubled lan', but we awlsuh knowed d'wahr's stuhrn truf d'man' ahr unyieldin' han'."

Lincoln's assassination encourages some southern cities of record to vehemently hold resentment in reserve toward government entitlements. Further racial and criminal attitudes amount to arrests that try to stifle guerilla gang actions and give stop to a multitude of scattered skirmishes. Notwithstanding the climate of the rest of the country, our nation's capital begins supplementary arrangements, which include high ranking officials, dignitaries and prominent citizens, as well as our newly sitting president and his cabinet. Andrew Johnson is unequivocally instrumental in modifying the mood of Washington D. C. after Lincoln's death. His thoughtful deliberation comes from inspecting a feck of soldier tents speckling the lawn's address. Nearing May's end the sanguine mind eventually relieves heavy hearted chests from all local citizens that come daily to pay respects.

The celebration rings with jovial gaiety for two days. Patriotic songs are sung by both soldiers and citizens, who assemble momentously enthused. Federal troops pass a reviewing stand in formal uniform dress, hundreds of men per hour, in order to honor each regiment his due. Many thousands progress in unison, while boisterous bands begin to hail weary warriors home with resounding tunes. President Johnson wants no Union soldier exempt from accolades, old or new.

Our heroes march to be acknowledged in exquisite view, unlike heading cross country to defy warfare's doom; they parade proudly the entire length of Pennsylvania's Avenue. Hats wave high during cheers from exuberant folks swarming streets, hanging out windows with the supreme show of garlanded flowers and clamoring atop roofs. Beautiful fabric draping bolsters the front and sides of the wood-hammered stand of Union blue. A distinguished panel sits or stands to honor the bypassing soldiers their long awaited due.

Jubilant of spirit they funnel through the city, proudly posturing as victorious troops. Quite an interminable procession of polished buttons and bayonets burnished with flickering flashes throughout the sunny laden queue. Long-standing acquaintances respark to hearty hand-shakes and a drink or two. Older friendships renew, when lockets with photo keepsakes and embroidered hankies are clasped in palms, love to rejuvenate. Families flourish again with long, amorous embraces due. They have been yearning for months or years to finally, intimately commune. Splendid the sky's banner with a glorious sunshine breaking through to administer issue for hours upon the brilliant blue, as it gives three armies chock allowance to pleasantly pass and receive their well-earned salutes.

Although a throng of freed blacks and a cattle herd terminate General Sherman's trailing tail, Lucy Higgs marches within the 23rd's companies, a leisurely smiling stride set huge. She carries her head high surrounded by rank and file of Indiana's cohorts and passes the dignitaries for review beaming a peaceful pride like a bride coming down the aisle in June.

"I s'pose muh head git buried deep in muh duties fo' awhile, cause I be nuhrsin', cookin' 'n' cleanin' cleah up d'coas' an' on up t'de Nawrth, but dat nex' yeahr o'mo' be a bluhr o'time… Dat's aw'ight. I feel a suhrge o'freedom's pride, when I gits t'walk wif awll dem so'jyuhs in d'p'rade an' heahr d'vic'try cries." As she scrunches up her shoulders in a smallish shrug, a light shines from within and she gives me the warmest smile. Little crinkles form right above the apples of her cheeks just under her deepset eyes. I too can't help but return with an added nod and a sympathetic smile.

SHARED STRIFE, FRIENDS FOR LIFE

By '65, lives and towns big and small rebuild in May and June, but for the most part, folks are just trying to pick themselves up by their bootstraps and continue. This leg of her journey now complete, nigh the pudding proves, but there is never a question as to what her New Albany, Indiana compatriots are going to do. They welcome their dear friend, "Aunt Lucy", to the place they call home to join them in building anew. She delves into housekeeping again with vigorous enthusiasm like she has done on furlough for a few. These same officers fully employ her at their residences on differing days by the first week in June.

"I'se ax't t'wuhrk ovuhr at d'houses o'two colonuhs for a second tour, Davis 'n' Hoopuh. From time t'time I checks in on d'Grisham family too, dey bein' neighbuhs an awll t'boot. Cawrse, he still be so lame wif shell shahrds t'de knee from some Rebuh foo'. Dat Missus be tryin' so hahrd t'be a good wife an' take care o'him, but she gots huhr han's full wif two babies, still so new. Missus Matilda approve me t'hep huhr out full time bout '78, which turn out a fine kettle o'stew. 'Vench'ly, Colonel Hoopuh remove' t'Kansas City… s'pose dat was 'bout '82."

Aunt Lucy nurse's at his side. He was quite a sight for sore eyes. The general had been poorly, since leaving the war wounded and he was well into the winter of his life. She settles into their employ for many years and grows closer as a friend to his wife. When Otto Gresham marries, Lucy arrives in Chicago for the wedding at the Palmer House as a family guest to watch their son betroth his bride.

Returning to, or in Lucy's case beginning, civilian life is the next rite of passage singularly paramount. While many of the saltier men go back to their steamboat trades of account, Lucy is content to lead a quiet life as a housekeeper, safe and sound. Other than patiently endearing herself to any ailing men of the 23rd living in New Albany or in the immediate area around, she mingles minimally within the community and finds a tiny cottage that suits her needs near the base of the Floyd Knobs on the outskirts of town. It is another veteran from the 23rd that catches her eye, the following summer of '66 on the Presbyterian Church grounds. While attending a Friday night fish fry and revival, he recognizes her, strolls on over and gives her a big beaming grin as he sits down.

John Nichols starts the Great Dispute as a fiddler, a taller, gentler musician whose kindness of character stands out. He joins the colored forces after the Vicksburg's furlough, when the Emancipation Proclamation Act is touted. He musters out as a private in '66, Company D of the colored troops, men from all around. Upon his valiant return to New Albany John becomes a fireman in town. His family and relations settled down, since 1840 as free blacks in New Albany and even earlier in Tennessee down south.

On a perfect April 13, day in 1870, a profoundly delightful ceremony takes place by the Presbyterian pastor and their legal, holy wedlock is announced. Lucy wears tiny, teardrop earrings and a crisp, collared frock with a belted blouse. They share much of their storied past, including the memory of Mo' by the meadow on high ground. The soldiers of the 23rd have moved many of their regiment to that same elevated spot down south.

"Yuh know, when I met Johnny, I ain't t'know he be Mo's fiddluh, ser'nadin' huhr grave an' suhpo'tin' muh side. Den, when I finds out who he be, it was a knee-slappin' suhrprise. Lawd sho' do wuhrk in a myster'ous style. Dey both been so good t'me awll dese yeahrs we suhrvived. We thanks d'Lawd he give us a go t'gethuh ev'ry day 'n' night. Sometime' I makes some pies 'n' teas fo' d'po', pale men still suff'rin' d'mut'latin' mis'ries o'war's plight. Johnny walks wif me t'de vet'ran' hospituh site. He hep me han' out some o'dem d'licious del'cacies an' den we prays 'n' sing some hymns o'he play fidduh fo' awhile."

Within these same five years from west to east, veterans stage get-togethers to relive battles and reunite. Colonel Sanderson of New Albany, Indiana is one of more than a hundred to apply for the Grand Army of the Republic organization for Civil War veterans and claim a site. An insular community of tightly bonded veterans now meets monthly to reminisce surviving the laborious fight, lobby to safeguard each others' rights and support each other's return to civilian life. It proves to be invaluable for the greater good of soldiers and their wives.

Lucy is unanimously elected for her service and noble nature during the war as an honorary member in one of their special rites. She travels to Indianapolis on occasion for the bigger meetings of posts within the state combined. Her entrance is always grand like a bride's receiving line. This formality makes her the only black, or female for that matter, in a GAR of men, unanimous election undenied.

During one of their get togethers in 1870, the assemblage ruminates about a steamboat trip to Vicksburg's bloody battle site. Many want to pay respects to those that lost their life. Lucy and John join the group to offer Mona's meadow tribute, to honor the fallen heroes there and give thanks to God who brought all out of such a dismal time. Outwardly, it appears to be simple, three day trip, but unknown to them any enemy, dreadful, deadly fomites, still lurks out of sight. Less than a week after returning, Lucy succumbs to the smallpox virus, preying rapidly vile.

A prepared room in another officer's home keeps her closely attended like family as her husband works two jobs during this fragile time. Everyday without missing a tic mark, most of the men who lived through her nursing attentions during the war, including Lorenzo and Charlie, come to call, read her passages from the Bible, steep healing sage tea for her and fluff and prop her pillow to pacify the weary nights. Finally, two week's worth of attentiveness and tea see reward on high. Their favored auntie, Lucy, survives a critical time.

~✦~

The 1892 act of congress finally allowed a nurse's pension, quite a blessing in Lucy's eyes. She asks the men to help her write a beautiful letter describing faithful service during the Civil War's fight. They write of her duties during the years in dispute, but the government wouldn't bite. All members of the Grand Army of the Republic's Sanderson Post are not only surprised, they are fit to be tied, when her pension application is denied. The GAR assists her as they do many veterans to apply for a pension's right. They continue to try as the example of true soldiering, does not give up the fight. As loyal as the day is long members entreat the government again with a petition signed by all the veterans still alive, to the tune of 55.

By '98 the hard earned pension is granted, regardless of the initial objection in spite. The retirement income is not only uncanny and wild, but some white women who nursed during that Great Dispute are unfortunately denied pension and do not have a company of men come to bat at their side. Magnanimously grateful to those who saved her life, not once, but twice, "Aunt Lucy" is finally able to step back and take a richly merited rest in life. Finally, after many years she is granted pay for her Civil War time.

I followed tabs on Lucy up to 1909, when her husband dies. Stroke's misery gives her another suffering time that implores the entire Sanderson Post of the Grand Army of the Republic to rush en masse to her bedside… and even that she survives. Truly Lucy Higgs-Nichols has a band of brothers and a guardian angel that consider her honorable and beloved as nurse, laundress, cook, mother and wife. Thanks to Providence for giving us Lucy Higgs Nichols' purpose beyond her repose of 1915 at the North Annex in His time… sublime.

EPILOGUE

Does a stamp of indemnity substitute honor for a forgotten soul strewn asunder, ghostly pale as laid? Ultimately, I hope to be a humble, blow horn's voice, modicum for the meek; and seen somewhat by social consideration, maimed. Folk tales retried in the name of acknowledged truth, not to slay the participants of Civil War's renowned stage, but to admonish those behind the scenes of the play, still exemplary in deed and homage, warranting of a history without regrets, if not fame… then verity unashamed. These points of interest from feasible, peasantries' patriotic witness duly pronounced become a foundling place. I chaffed at the bit like a hopeful horse just happy to be on the field of the Derby's cavalcade.

I had challenged fate to find someone inspiring change, a person that meets glory and danger alike, yet shines on, surprisingly brave. Decidedly earnest, I wished as well to convey firm evidence of a simpler folk sporting integrity's case, though possibly displaced and often tempered or nullified, in respect to that which is hidden by society's louder complaints. Providence pulled rank from within, trying to recalibrate the country's spiritual gage. An insignificant pebble's purpose in grand design shall affect the rippled water's break. A small convincing picture, but illustrative of scrutiny to the suitable sketch of those deserving the honor of a nation's praise. So many stalwart sent sacrificed their all and never sought fame, yet heretofore remembered least or remaining—unnamed.

My penchant for wielding pen, not sword, as a mighty weapon to elucidate was bridled upon prospect, because glory will always fade. I ascertain of the people and places purposed in my assigned domain this one woman's story in New Albany, Indiana kept burning in my brain. Lucy Higgs-Nichols divulged her life to me with vulnerability, yet a spirit as courageous as a mountain lion never untamed. Running the gambit from suffering to joy and back to pain she spoke, with scintillating side notes and melodious strains. A privileged perspective was gained from people unwavering in faith. This is a hope I maintain as the story of Lucy Higgs-Nichols sparked anew in me a spiritual flame. An experience which emboldened my ability for love and to this day remains. In life's journey, slivers of a soul strewn apart or buried deep still sparkle in the shards. Collected pieces from the present to the start see God's purpose shine afar like a polished patina, never lying down nor asleep with stars, while a soul's truth, left to impart, shatters a lonely darkness to lighten the heart.

PENSION FOR LUCY NICHOLS.

Noted Woman Warrior from Ohio Receives Her Reward.

NEW ALBANY, Ind., Dec. 13.—Aunt Lucy Nichols of this city has just been granted a pension of $12 per month by special act of Congress. She is the only female member of the Grand Army of the Republic post in the United States. She served through the war with the Twenty-third Indiana, participating in twenty-eight battles. She fought, nursed the sick, and cooked and washed for the officers. She joined the regiment at Bolivar, Tenn., having run away from her master. He traced her to the camp of the Twenty-third, but she begged protection, and the soldiers kept her. Her daughter, who was with her, died at Vicksburg. Lucy was with the regiment at Washington when it was mustered out, and accompanied the men to New Albany.

This photo is one of the only known photos of Lucy Higgs Nichols taken in 1898 during a reunion of the Grand Army of the Republic, when they met in Indianapolis, Indiana. She stands with the men and her cane in the center.

Permissions: *Photo of Lucy Higgs Nichols used by permission of the Stuart B. Wrege Indiana History Room, New Albany – Floyd County Public Library

REFERENCES

NEWSPAPERS

Various Articles, Harper's Weekly, 01/05/1861–12/30/1865. *"The Battle Of Pittsburgh Landing," New York Herald-Tribune*, 04/10/1862.

"Daughter Of The Regiment," *Janesville Daily Gazette*, 03/14/1889, P.1

"Negro Woman Given Membership In G.A.R.," *Atlanta Constitution*, 01/31/1891.

"Gray Heads And Gray Beards In Reunion," *New Albany Daily Ledger*, 09/21/ 1894.

"Colored Nurse's Pension," *Logansport Journal*, 07/15/1898, P.5

"Noted Woman Warrior Receives Her Reward," *New York Times*, 12/14/1898.

"Why Aunt Lucy Got A Pension," *The Denver Sunday Post*, 12/18/1898.

"Negress Who Nursed Soldiers Is A Member Of The G. A. R.," *The Freeman*, 09/03/1904.

"Only Woman Ever Member Of G.A.R. Dies In Asylum," *New Albany Daily Ledger*, 01/29/1915.

Lucy Nichols In "Obituary Notes," *New York Times*, 01/31/1915.

Lucy Nichols Article, *New Albany Weekly Ledger*, 02/03/1915.

Shiels, Damain, "Who Shot General Mcpherson," *Civil War Gazette*, 02/01/2001.

Bean, Amanda, "The Civil War: 23[Rd] Indiana Regiment," *News And Tribune*, 03/13/2013.

Bean, Amanda, "The Civil War: Lucy Higgs Nichols," News And Tribune, 03/20/2013.

BOOKS

Edmonds, S. Emma E., Nurse And Spy. W. S. Williams & Co. 1865.

Findling, John, A History Of New Albany, Indiana. Indiana University Southeast, 2003.

Funk, Arville L., A Sketchbook Of Indiana History. Rochester, Indiana: Christian Book Press, 1969, Revised 1983.

Holland, Mary A. Gardner, Our A.M. Nurses. Boston: B. Wilkins & Co. 1895

Grant, Ulysses S., *Personal Memoirs Of U. S. Grant*. Charles L. Webster & Company, 1885–86.Isbn: 0-914427-67-9.

Hanson, Kathleen S., "Down To Vicksburg: The Nurses' Experience", Journal Of The Illinois State Historical Society, 06/01/2005. Isbn: 1522-1067.

Hooper, Shadrach K.,A Historical Sketch Of The 23Rd Indiana Volunteer Infantry July 29Th, 1861, To July 23Rd, 1865, Report Of The Indiana-Vicksburg Military Park Commission, 1910, Prepared In Pamphlet Form By The Author For Private Distribution To The Survivors Of The 23Rd Indiana Regiment At Their Annual Reunion, New Albany, Indiana, 09/29-30/1910.

Loughborough, Mary Ann, My Cave Life In Vicksburg With Letters Of Trial And Travel, By A Lady. New York: D. Appleton & Co., 1864.

Peters, Pamela R., Peters, Curtis H., And Meginity, Victor C., "Lucy Higgs Nichols," Traces, Winter 2010.

DOCUMENTS AND RECORDS

The National Archives, Soldier's Certificate No. 975436

The National Archives, Us Colored Troops Military Service Records, Film 3M589

The Civil War Archive – Indiana Units

Amazing Grace Lyrics, John Newton (1725-1807)

Floyd County, Indiana, Index To Marriage Record 1845-1920

Inclusive Volume W. P. A. Book Number Indicates Location Of Record, Book 6, P. 572.

Caron's Directory Of The City Of New Albany 1888-1889 Halifax County Deed Books, Bk. 22, P. 225,

No. 24 United States Federal Census Records, 1830,1840,1850,1860,1870,1880,1890

Hardeman County, Tennessee Records, Inventory Of Rueben Higgs' Slave Property, 03/02/ 1846

Hardeman County, Tennessee Records, Inventory Of Rueben Higgs' Slave Property, 07/09/ 1855

Hardeman County, Tennessee Records, Index To Marriage Record January 1866

Floyd County, Indiana, General Affidavit For Claim No. 1130541, 29/07/1993

Floyd County, Indiana, Pension Office, Deposition #6, Case Of Lucy Nichols, No. 1130541, 04/12/1894

55[Th] Congress, 2[Nd] Session, H. R. Report No. 4741 {To Accompany H.R. 1366}, 06/23/1898

WEBSITES

http://www.sonofthesouth.net/leefoundation/civil-war/1862/corinth-mississippi-battle.htm

http:/www.civilwarindex.com/armyin/officers/23rd_in_infantry_officers.pdf

http://www.carnegiecenter.org/docs/cc-lucy_curriculum_090412-4.pdf

http://www.cityofbolivar.info/the%20history%20of%20bolivar

http://www.civilwarindex.com/armyin/soldiers/23rd_in_infantry_soldiers.pdf

http://www.in.gov/dnr/historic/files/newalbany.pdf

http://www.nafclibrary.org/resources/adults/indiana/service/23rdindianavolunteer.pdf

http://www30.us.archive.org/stream/indianaatvicksbu00indi#page/n5/mode/2up

http://www.uky.edu/libraries/nkaa/record.php?note_id=2435

http://www.waymarking.com/waymarks/wma2v7_wexford_lodge_shirley_house_civil_war_vicksburg_mswexford lodge (shirley house)–civil war–vicksburg, ms–field hospitals, vicksburg national military park, 3201 clay street, vicksburg, ms 39183,usa.

http://www.bitsofblueandgray.com/morgan.htm letters of william curtis morgan 23rd indiana volunteers

http://archive.org/stream/lifeofwalterquin01gres#page/n33/mode/2up gresham, matilda Life Of Walter Quintin Gresham, 1832-1895.

http://en.wikipedia.org/wiki/indiana_in_the_american_civil_war

http://en.wikipedia.org/w/index.php?title=23rd-indiana-volunteer-infantry-regiment&oldid=399464341

http://en.wikipedia.org/wiki/grand_review_of_the_armies

http://www.civilwar.org/battlefields/vicksburg/vicks-
burg-history-articles/vicksburgwinshcelhg.html

http://militaryhistory.about.com/od/army/ig/
selected-union-generals/

BIBLIOGRAPHY

BOOKS

Ahlstrome, Sydney E., America *A Religious History of the American People*, Yale University Press, 1972.

Ballard, *Michael B.*, "Iuka: A Strange Civil War Battle in Northeast Mississippi, *"Mississippi Historical Society © 2000–2013.*

Ballard, Michael B., "Vicksburg during the Civil War (1862-1863): A Campaign; A Siege," Mississippi Historical *Society © 2004.*

Ballard, Michael B. *Civil War Mississippi: A Guide.* Jackson: University Press of Mississippi, 2000.

Bellows, Henry W., Brockett, Linus P. Vaughan, Mary, "Women's Work in the Civil War: A Record of Heroism, Patriotism, and Patience", Zeigler, McCurdy & Company, 1867.

Dunaway, Wilma A.," The African-American Family in Slavery and Emancipation". Virginia Polytechnic Institute and State University Series: Studies in Modern Capitalism, June 2003. ISBN: 9780521012164.

Eicher, David J., the Longest Night: A Military History of the Civil War. New York: Simon & Schuster, 2001. ISBN: 0-684-84944-5.

Foulke, William D., Life of Oliver P. Morton. Bowen-Merrill Company, 1899.

Hoeling, A.H., et. al., eds. *Vicksburg: 47 Days of Siege May 18-July 4, 1863*. Englewood Cliffs, New Jersey: Prentice-Hall, Inc., 1969.

Leidner, Gordon, "Religious Revival in Civil War Armies," Great American History

Peters, Pamela R., "The Underground Railroad in Floyd County, Indiana," Jefferson, N.C.: McFarland & Co., Inc., 2001.

Simon, John Y., the *Papers of Ulysses S. Grant*, Vol. 8 *April 1 – July 6, 1863* Carbondale: Southern Illinois University Press, 1979, ISBN: 0-8093-0884-3.

WINSce, TERRENCE J., "Vicksburg Campaign: Unvexing the Father of Waters", Rand, McNally & Company, Chicago 1919.

Woodworth, Steven E., *Nothing but Victory: The Army of the Tennessee, 1861–1865*. New York: Alfred A. Knopf, 2005, ISBN 0-375-41218-2.

WEBSITES

http://archive.org/details/ourarmynursesint00holl

http://www.kidport.com/reflib/usahistory/civilwar/CampLife.htm

http://www.google.com/search?q=descriptions+of+ci
vil+war+camp+life&hl=en&qscrl=1&rlz=1T4M
XGB_enUS521US521&tbm=isch&tbo=u&sour
ce=univ&sa=X&ei=CzhEUYrMKYfHrQGji4Cg
BA&ved=0CC0QsAQ&biw=911&bih=427

http://www.tngenweb.org/records/hardeman/history/
goodspeed/bios.html#higgs

http://library.mtsu.edu/tps/Women_and_the_Civil_
War.pdf

http://archive.org/stream/
civilwarletterso00hard#page/n195/mode/1up

http://archive.org/stream/civilwarletters00#page/n12/
mode/1up

http://dig.lib.niu.edu/ISHS/ishs-2004winter/ishs-
2004winter286.pdf

http://www.idaillinois.org/cdm/compoundobject/
collection/isl7/id/965

http://www.artcirclelibrary.info/Reference/civil-
war/1862-08.pdf

http://en.wikipedia.org/wiki/
Music_of_the_American_Civil_War

http://www.sallysfamilyplace.com/Neighbors/Griffith.
htm

http://oldcourthouse.org/phototour.htm

http://www.newsinhistory.com/feature/battle-shiloh-
bloody-civil-war-clash-shocks-america

http://www.mycivilwar.com/facts/usa/usa-medical.
html

http://mshistorynow.mdah.state.ms.us/articles/215/
vicksburg-during-the-civil-war-1862-1863

http://www.idsnews.com/812magazine/?p=10224

http://en.wikipedia.org/wiki/Battle_of_Corydon

http://audio38.archive.org/details/civilwarletters00

http://archive.org/details/civilwarletterso00hard

http://www.gardenguides.com/91875-native-plants-
mississippi.html

http://en.wikipedia.org/wiki/
List_of_birds_of_Indiana

http://www.ehow.com/info_8503979_native-plants-
birds-tennessee.html